PASTIME STORIES

BY

THOMAS NELSON PAGE

ILLUSTRATED BY A. B. FROST

Short Story Index Reprint Series

BOOKS FOR LIBRARIES PRESS
FREEPORT, NEW YORK

First published 1894
Reprinted 1969

Standard Book Number: 8369-3009-6

LIBRARY OF CONGRESS CATALOG CARD NUMBER:

76-75784

TO

ALL GOOD STORY-TELLERS

WHO HAVE SWEETENED LIFE
WITH THEIR HUMOR

PREFACE

It used to be the custom for a writer on coming before the public to address a word to the "gentle reader," a custom which had this double advantage: that the author had his "word," and the reader, on his side, was not obliged to hear it. I wish now to avail myself of this old custom, and my gentle readers, if such there shall be, may take advantage of their privilege also. I will simply say that no one will be as sensible of the demerits of these stories as I am myself. So, my "gentle reader," we agree on that point at least. If you ask me why, then, I wrote them, I will say truthfully, because I was asked and chose to do so. Then, why did I publish them? Because I found a publisher.

There are some good stories in the lot, old stories which have survived for generations—one, I am satisfied, for at least a century—and if they do not read well, it is because I have marred them in the telling. This is as much my misfortune as yours; so do not complain, when I have tried to entertain you. The only persons who have that right are my friends, Major J. Horace Lacy, Connelly F. Trigg, Polk Miller, Henry W. Hobson, William F. Gordon, Jr., and a few others, who told me stories too good to be lost, whether I have been able to preserve them or not.

I must make my acknowledgments to "Porte Crayon" for an incident in "Rachel's Lovers;" and if, "gentle reader," I can excite your curiosity so far as to make you go back to that early and delightful chronicle of old Virginia life, you will owe me a debt of gratitude which will offset all my deficiencies.

Thos. Nelson Page.

CONTENTS

	PAGE
OLD SUE	3
HOW JINNY EASED HER MIND	10
ISRUL'S BARGAIN	23
THE TRUE STORY OF THE SURRENDER OF THE MARQUIS CORNWALLIS	34
WHEN LITTLE MORDECAI WAS AT THE BAR	41
CHARLIE WHITTLER'S CHRISTMAS PARTY	51
HOW RELIUS "BOSSED THE RANCH"	63
THE PROSECUTION OF MRS. DULLET	70
ONE FROM FOUR	79
THE DANGER OF BEING TOO THOROUGH	86
UNCLE JACK'S VIEWS OF GEOGRAPHY	92
BILLINGTON'S VALENTINE	97
SHE HAD ON HER GERANIUM LEAVES	110
A STORY OF CHARLES HARRIS	117
HE WOULD HAVE GOTTEN A LAWYER	121
HOW ANDREW CARRIED THE PRECINCT	127
"RASMUS"	143

	PAGE
HER SYMPATHETIC EDITOR	149
HE KNEW WHAT WAS DUE TO THE COURT	160
HER GREAT-GRANDMOTHER'S GHOST	168
RACHEL'S LOVERS	182
JOHN'S WEDDING SUIT	198
WHEN THE COLONEL WAS A DUELLIST	209

ILLUSTRATIONS

THE MULE AT HIS HEELS	*Facing page*	7
HOW JINNY EASED HER MIND	" "	14
"'GOOD EVE'NIN', MARSE SATAN'"	" "	32
"'I IS DE SON OF DE AMERICAN REBELUTION'"	" "	36
"'HE RIZ JES' A P'INT, JES' ONE P'INT'"	" "	50
"'I HAVE GOT A DROP OF THE IRISH IN ME, MESELF'"	" "	60
"'YOU HAS DONE COMMIT A PENITENTIARY OFFENCE'"	" "	72
BUYING THE WEDDING-RING	" "	84
"SOME ONE BEHIND ME SAID, 'HOLD ON!'"	" "	90
"'TAKE OFF YOUR COAT'"	" "	94
"'I FOUND HER A BUNCH OF APPLE BLOSSOMS'"	" "	100
"HE WAS AS MELLOW AS AN APPLE"	" "	114
"'YOUR PA NEVER WOULD STOOD NO SICH THING AS DAT'"	" "	118
"'EF I HAD, I'D 'A' GOT ME A LAWYER'"	" "	124
"'YOU COLD? I'LL WARM YOU'"	" "	134
"'YOU KNOWS DEM CRUEL S'CIETY ANIMALS IS LOOKIN' ROUND'"	" "	146
"'WHICH IS THE EDITOR?'"	" "	156

"HE WAS NOT EXACTLY A VAGABOND" . . .	*Facing page*	162
"I BECAME GRADUALLY CONSCIOUS OF A PRESENCE"	" "	178
"'EF YOU'S A RAT, I'LL KNOW YOU'" . . .	" "	196
"HE LOOKED AT HIMSELF SOLEMNLY"	" "	202
"'I WAS IN LINDMAN'S BED'"	" "	218

PASTIME STORIES

OLD SUE

JUST on the other side of Ninth Street, outside of my office window, was the stand of Old Sue, the "tug-mule" that pulled the green car around the curve from Main Street to Ninth and up the hill to Broad. Between her and the young bow-legged negro that hitched her on, drove her up, and brought her back down the hill for the next car there always existed a peculiar friendship. He used to hold long conversations with her, generally upbraiding her in that complaining tone with opprobrious terms which the negroes employ, which she used to take meekly. At times he petted her with his arm around her neck, or teased her, punching her in the ribs, and walking about around her quarters, ostentatiously disregardful of her switching stump of a tail,

backed ears, and uplifted foot, and threatening her with all sorts of direful punishment if she "jis dyarred to tetch" him. "Kick me—heah, kick me; I jis dyah you to lay you' foot 'g'inst me," he would say, standing defiantly against her as she appeared about to let fly at him. Then he would seize her with a guffaw. Or at times, coming down the hill, he would "haul off" and hit her, and "take out" with her at his heels, her long furry ears backed, and her mouth wide open as if she would tear him to pieces; and just as she nearly caught him he would come to a stand and wheel around, and she would stop dead, and then walk on by him as sedately as if she were in a harrow. In all the years of their association she never failed him; and she never failed to fling herself on the collar, rounding the sharp curve at Ninth, and to get the car up the difficult turn.

Last fall, however, the road passed into new hands, and the management changed the old mules on the line, and put on a lot of new and green horses. It happened to be a dreary, rainy day in November when the first new team was put in. They came along about three o'clock. Old Sue had been standing out in the pouring rain all day with her head bowed, and her stubby tail tucked in, and her black back dripping. She had never failed nor faltered. The tug-boy, in an old rubber suit and battered tarpauling hat, had been out also, his coat shining with the wet. He and Old Sue appeared to mind it astonishingly little. The gutters were running brimming full, and the cobble-stones were wet and slippery. The street cars were crowded inside and out, the wretched people on the platforms vainly trying to shield themselves with umbrellas held sideways. It was late in the afternoon when I first observed that there was trouble at the corner. I thought at first that there was an accident, but soon found that it was due to a pair of new, balking horses in a car. Old Sue was hitched to the tug, and was doing her part faithfully; finally she threw her weight on the collar, and by sheer strength bodily dragged the car, horses and all, around the curve and on up the straight track, until the horses, finding themselves moving, went off with a rush. I saw the tug-boy shake his head with pride, and heard him give a whoop of triumph. The next car went up all right;

but the next had a new team, and the same thing occurred. The streets were like glass; the new horses got to slipping and balking, and Old Sue had to drag them up as she did before. From this time it went from bad to worse: the rain changed to sleet, and the curve at Ninth became a stalling-place for every car. Finally, just at dark, there was a block there, and the cars piled up. I intended to have taken a car on my way home, but finding it stalled, I stepped into my friend Polk Miller's drug-store, just on the corner, to get a cigar and to keep warm. I could see through the blurred glass of the door the commotion going on just outside, and could hear the shouts of the driver and of the tug-boy mingled with the clatter of horses' feet as they reared and jumped, and the cracks of the tug-boy's whip as he called to Sue, "Git up, Sue; git up, Sue." Presently, I heard a shout, and then the tones changed, and things got quiet.

A minute afterwards the door slowly opened, and the tug-boy came in limping, his old hat pushed back on his head, and one leg of his wet trousers rolled up to his knee, showing about four inches of black, ashy shin, which he leaned over and rubbed as he walked. His wet face wore a scowl, half pain, half anger. "Mist' Miller, kin I use yo' telephone?" he asked, surlily. (The company had the privilege of using it by courtesy.)

"Yes; there 'tis."

He limped up, and still rubbing his leg with one hand, took the 'phone off the hook with the other and put it to his ear.

"Hello, central — hello! Please gimme fo' hund' an' sebenty-three on three sixt'-fo'— fo' hund' an' sebent'-three on three sixt'-fo'.

Hello!—Suh? Yas, suh; fo' hund' an' sebent'-three on three sixt'-fo'. *Street-car stables* on three sixt'-fo'. Hello! hello! Hello! Dat you, street-car stables? Hello! Yas. Who dat? Oh! Dat you, Mis' Mellerdin? Yas, suh; yes, suh; Jim; *Jim;* dis Jim. G-i-m, Jim. Yas, suh: Jim, whar drive Ole Sue, in Mis' Polk Miller' drug-sto'. Yas, suh; yas, suh. Suh? Yas, suh. Oh! Mis' Mellerdin, kin I git off to-night? Suh? Yas, suh. 'Matter'? — Ole Sue — she done tu'n fool; done gone 'stracted. I can't do nuttin 'tall wid her. She ain' got no sense. She oon pull a poun'. Suh? Yas, suh. Nor, suh. Yas, suh. Nor, suh; I done try ev'ything. I done beg her, done cuss her, done whup her mos' to death. She ain' got no reasonment. She oon do nuttin. She done haul off, an' leetle mo' knock my brains out; she done kick me right 'pon meh laig — 'pon my right laig." (He stooped over and rubbed it again at the reflection.) " Done bark it all up. Suh? Yas, suh. Tell nine o'clock? Yas, suh; reckon so; 'll try it leetle longer. Yas, suh; yas, suh. Good-night—good-bye!"

He hung the 'phone back on the hook,

stooped and rolled down the leg of his breeches. "Thankee, Mist' Miller! Good-night."

He walked to the door, and opened it. As he passed slowly out, without turning his head, he said, as if to himself, but to be heard by us, "I wish I had a hunderd an' twenty-five dollars. I boun' I'd buy dat durned ole mule, an' cut her doggoned th'oat."

HOW JINNY EASED HER MIND

Uncle Ben Williamson was as well known in town as the mayor or the governor. He was an "old-time darky," and to this character owed his position, which was a good one. He had been "Boy" about law offices in the Law Building ever since the first evening some years before when he had knocked gently at Judge Allen's door, and then, after a tardy invitation, had slipped slowly in sideways, with his old beaver hat in his hand, and, having taken in in his comprehensive glance the whole room, including the Judge himself, had said, apparently satisfied, that he had heard they wanted a boy, and he wanted a place. It was an auspicious moment for the old fellow; the last "boy," a drunkard and a thief, had just been discharged, and the judge had been much worried that day trying to wait on himself. His thoughts had turned in the waning evening light to his home, from which the light had faded for all time, and his heart was softened. The old lawyer had looked Ben over too, and been satisfied. Something about him had called up tender recollections of his little office at the old Court-house before he became a successful lawyer and a celebrated judge, and when his best friend was the old drunken negro who waited on him, "cleaned up" (?) his room, and was his principal client and most sympathetic friend and counsellor in his long love-affair with his sweetheart, the old colonel's brown-eyed daughter. He had just been dreaming of her, first as she wore his first violets, and then as she lay for the last time, with her head pillowed in his roses, and her white, slender hands, whiter than ever, clasped over his last violets on her quiet breast.

He had recalled all the sweet difficulties in winning her; his falling back into dissipation, his picking himself up again, and again his failure; and then the lonely evening when he had sat in front of the dying fire, sad, despairing, and had wondered if life were worth holding longer; then old William slipping in, hat in hand. He recalled the old man's keen look

at him as he sat before the fire with the pistol half hidden under the papers on his desk, and his sudden breaking of the silence with :
"Don't you give her up, Marse Johnny; don't you nuver give her up. Ef she's wuth havin', she's wuth fightin' for; an' ef she say No, she jes beginnin' to mean Yes. Don't you give her up." And he had not given her up, and she had called him from the dead and had made him. He would not have given the right to put those violets in her calm hands for a long life of unbroken happiness with any one else. So, when the door opened quietly, and Uncle Ben, in his clean shirt, time-browned coat, and patched breeches, slipped in, it was an auspicious moment for him.

"Where did you come from?" he asked him.

"From old Charlotte, suh; used to 'longst to de Bruces."

"Can you clean up?"

He laughed a spontaneous, jolly laugh. "Kin I clean up? Dat's what I come to do. Jinny ken, too."

"Can you read?"

"Well, nor, suh, not edzactly. I ain't no free-issue nigger ner preacher." The shade of disappointment on his face counterbalanced this, however.

" Do you get drunk ?"

"Yes, sir, sometimes."—Cheerfully. " Not so often. I 'ain't got nuttin to git de whiskey. But ef I's drunk, Jinny cleans up."

" Who is Jinny ?"

" She's my wife."

" What sort of a woman is she ?"

" She's a black woman. Oh!—she's a good sort o' ooman—a toler'ble good sort o' ooman, ef you know how to git 'long wid her. Sort o' raspy sometimes, like urr wimmens, but I kin manage her. You kin try us. Ef you don't like us we ken go. We 'ain't got no root to we foots."

" You'll do. I'll try you," said the judge; and from that time Uncle Ben became the custodian of the offices. He was a treasure. As he had truly said, he got drunk sometimes, but when he did, Jinny took his place and cleaned up. Her temper was, as he had said, certainly " raspy." Even flattery must have admitted this, and Uncle Ben wore a bandage or plaster on some part of his head a considerable part of his time; but no one ever heard him complain. "Jinny jes been kind o' easin' her mine," he said, in answer to questions.

At length it culminated: one night Jinny went to work on him with a flat-iron to such good purpose that first a policeman came in, and then a doctor had to be called to bring him to, and Jinny was arrested.

Next morning, when Jinny was sent on to the grand jury for striking with intent to maim, disfigure, disable, and kill, Ben was a trifle triumphant. When the justice announced his decision, he rose, and shaking his long finger at her, exclaimed, " Aye, aye, what I tell you?"

"Silence!" roared the big tipstaff, and Ben sat down with a puzzled look on his face.

When the police court closed he went up to his wife, and said, in a commanding tone: "Now come 'long home wid me an' 'have yourself. I'll teach you to sling flat-iron at folks' head!"

The officer announced, however, that Jinny would have to go to jail—the case had passed beyond his jurisdiction. She had been "sent on to the grand jury."

Ben's countenance fell. "Got to go to jail!"

HOW JINNY EASED HER MIND

he repeated, mechanically, in a dazed kind of way. " Got to go to jail!" Then the prisoners were taken down to the jail. He followed behind the line of stragglers that generally attended that interesting procession, and he sat on a stone outside the iron door nearly all day.

That afternoon he spent in the judge's office. The grand jury was in session, and next day "a true bill" was found against Jinny Williamson for an attempt to maim, disfigure, disable, and kill—a felony. The same day her case was called, the first on the docket.

She had good counsel. She could have had every lawyer in the building had she wanted them, so efficiently had old Ben polled the bar. But the case was a dead open-and-shut one. Unhappily, the judge was ill with gout. The Commonwealth called Ben, first man, and he told simply the same story he had told at the police court and to the grand jury. Jinny had always had a vicious temper, and had often exercised it towards him. That evening she had gone rather far, and finally he had attempted to remonstrate with her, had " tapped her with his open hand," and she had pounded his head with the flat-iron. The officer was called, and corroborated the story. He had heard the noise; had gone in and found Ben unconscious, and the woman in a fury, swearing to kill him. The surgeon pronounced the wound one which came near being very serious; but for Ben's exceptionally hard head, the skull would have been fractured; as it was, only the outer plate of the frontal bone was broken. He had known several men killed by blows much less vigorous. No cross-examination affected the witnesses. Ben had evidently told his story unwillingly. The jury was solemn. Earnest if short speeches were made. The judge gave a strong instruction upon the evil of women being lawless and murderous, and the jury retired. The counsel leaned over and told Ben he thought they had lost the case, and the jury would probably send his wife up for at least a year. Ben said nothing. He only looked once at Jinny sitting sullen and lowering in the prisoners' box beside a thief. Then, after a while, he got up and went out, and a minute later slipped in again at the door sideways, and making his way over to her, put an orange—not a very large or fresh one—into her lap. She did not look at him.

The appearance of the jury filing in glum and important sent him to his seat. The clerk called the names and asked, "Gentlemen of the jury, have you agreed on a verdict?" The consumptive-looking foreman bowed, and handed in the indictment, amid a sudden silence, and the clerk read, slowly, "We, the jury, find the prisoner guilty," etc., "and sentence her to confinement in the penitentiary for two years." Neither Jinny nor Ben stirred, nor did the counsel. He was evidently considering. The judge, in a voice slightly troubled, said he would pronounce sentence at once, and asked the prisoner if she had anything she wished to say. She rocked a little and glanced shyly over towards Ben with a sort of appealing look—her first—; said nothing, looked down again, and turned her orange over in her lap.

"Stand up," said the judge; and she stood up.

Just then Ben stood up too, and making his way over to her, said, "Jedge, ken I say a wud?"

"Why—ah—yes," said the judge, doubtfully. "It is very unusual, but go on." He sat back in his arm-chair.

"Well, gent'mens," began Ben, " I jes wants to say " (he paused, and took in the entire court-room in the sweep of his glance)—" I jes wants to say dat I don't think you ought to do Jinny dat a-way. Y'all 'ain' got nuttin 't all 'ginst Jinny. She 'ain' do nuttin to you all —nuttin 't all. She's my wife, an' what she done she done to me. Ef I kin stan' it, y'all ought to be able to, dat's sho'. Now hit's dis a-way. Y'all is married gent'mens, an' yo' knows jes how 'tis. Yo' knows sometimes a ooman gits de debil in her. 'Tain't her fault; 'tis de debil's. Hit jes like wolf in cows. Sometimes dee gits in de skin an' mecks 'em kick up an' run an' mean. Dat's de way 'tis wid wimmens. I done know Jinny ever sence she wuz a little gal at home in de country. I done know how mean she is. I done know all dat, an' I done marry her, 'cuz she suit me. I had plenty o' urr gals I could 'a' marry, but I ain' want dem. I want Jinny, an' I pester her tell she had me. Well, she meaner eben 'n I think she is; but dat ain' nuttin: I satisfied wid her, an' dat's 'nough. Y'all don' know how mean she is. She mean as a narrer-faced mule. She kick an' she fight an' she quoil tell sometimes I hardly ken stay in muh house; but dat ain' nuttin. I stay dyah, an' when she git thoo I right dyah jes same as befo', an' I know den I gwine have a good supper, an' I ain' got to pester my mine 'bout nuttin. Y'all done been all 'long dyah, 'cuz y'all is married gent'mens. Well, dat's de way 'twuz turr night. Jinny been good so long, I feared she got some'n de matter wid her, an' I kind o' git oneasy, an' sort o' poke her up. But she ain't; she all right. I so glad to find her dat way, I sort o' uppish, an' when she hit me I slapped her. I didn' mean to hu't her; I jes hit her a little tap side her head, so, an' she went all to pieces in a minute. I done hurt her feelin's. Y'all knows how 'tis yo'self. Wimmen's got mighty cu'ious feelin's, ain' like chillern's nor men's. Ef you slap 'em, dey goes dat a-way. Dey gits aggervated, an' den dey got to ease dee mine. Well, Jinny she got mighty big mine, an' when she dat a-way it tecks right smart to ease it—to smoove it. Fust she done try broom, den cheer, den shovel, den skillet; but ain' none o' dem able to ease her, an' den she got to try de flat-iron. She got to do it. Y'all knows how 'tis. Ef wimmen's got to do anything dey got to do it, an' dat's all. Flatiron don' hu't none. I 'ain' eben feel it. Hit jes knock me out muh head little while, an' I jes good as I wuz befo'. When I come to I fine dee done 'rest Jinny. Dat's what hu't me. Jinny done been easin' her mine all dese years, an' we 'ain' nuver had no trouble befo'. An' now y'all say she got to go to de pen'tentia'y. How'd y'all like somebody to sen' you' wife to pen'tentia'y when she jes easin' her mine? I ax you dat. How she gwine ease her mine dyah? I ax you dat. I know y'all gwine sen' her dyah, gent'mens, 'cuz you done say you is. I know you is, an' I 'ain' got nuttin to say 'bout it, not a wud; but all I ax you is to le' me go dyah too. I don' want stay here b'dout Jinny, an' y'all ain' gwine to know how to manage her b'dout me. I is de on'iest one kin do dat. Jinny got six chillern—little chillern—dis las' crap; she didn' hab none some sevrul years, an' den she had six. I gwine bring 'em all right up heah to y'all to teck keer on, 'cuz I gwine wid her—ef you le' me. I kyarn stan' it dyah by myself. I leetle mo' went 'stracted last night. Y'all kin have 'em, 'cuz y'all ken teck keer on 'em, an' I kyan't. I would jes like you to let her go home for a leetle while 'fo' yo' sen' her up, I jes would like dat. She got a right new baby dyah squealin' for her dis minute, an' I mighty feared hit gwine to die widout her, an' dat 'll be right hard 'pon Jinny. She 'ain' never los' but byah one, an' I had right smart trouble wid her 'bout dat. She sort o' out her head arter dat some sevrul months, till she got straight agin. I git 'long toler'ble well wid de urr chillerns, but I ain' able to nuss dat new one, an' she squeal all night. I got a ooman to come dyah an' look arter it, but she say she want Jinny, an' I think Jinny want her—I think she do. Jes let her go dyah a little while. Dat's all I want to ax you."

He sat down.

A glance at Jinny proved his assertion. Her eyes were shut fast, and with her arms tightly folded across her ample bosom, she was rocking gently from side to side. Two tears had pushed out from under her eyes, and stood gleaming on her black cheeks.

The counsel glanced up at the judge, whose face wore a look of deep perplexity, and then at the jury. "I would like to poll the jury," he said.

The clerk read the verdict over, and called the first name. " Is that your verdict ?"

The juror arose. " Well, judge, I thought it was; but " (he looked down at his fellows) " I think if I could I would like to talk to one or two of the other jurors a minute, if it is not too late. My wife's got a right new baby at home herself that squealed a little last night, and I'd like to go back to the room and think about it."

" Sheriff, take the jury back to their room," said the judge, firmly.

In a few minutes they returned, and the verdict was read :

" We, the jury, all married men, find the prisoner guilty of only easing her mind."

ISRUL'S BARGAIN

WHEN I was at college after the war, clothing was very scarce; there was not a dress suit in college, and very few new suits of any kind. I remember my best coat was made out of an old cloth skirt of my mother's. Billy Logan, however, tall and blond, was a swell, and in his third year he turned up with a brand-new suit: long frock-coat, lavender trousers, and a beaver hat that was dazzling. He was simply "a howler," and caught Miss Mabel, the Doctor's pretty daughter, "out of hand."

"Isrul" was the fiddler of the town (as black as your boot), and though he could not make a small city a great one, he could play the fiddle. He was also a drunkard and a thief. He and Billy Logan were great friends. He considered himself a swell also. But the night before the 1st of April, 1869 (on which night we always had a calathump, followed the next night by "a ball"), Isrul was sulky, owing partly to a recent and powerful sermon against fiddling, by the Rev. Amos Brown, and partly to a difference they had had about a dusky "sister" in the Rev. Amos's congregation, in which the Rev. Amos had come off victor. When we, as usual, approached him about the music for "the ball," he announced that he had "done gin up fiddlin' and gone to seekin'." It took several stiff drinks from a large bottle, obtained for the festivities by Billy Logan, and a sight of Billy's new suit to soften him. Billy, a little mellow, even put the suit on to show him how he would look when he should lead his partner up the floor to his music. Up to the top of the room he swaggered, turned with a swing, shouted, in Isrul's tone, "S'lute your pardners," and gave a long, low bow as he lifted the bottle to his lips.

Isrul's countenance relaxed. "Umh!" he declared. "Whar meh fiddle? Ef I jest had a coat and pyah o' breeches like dem, I could outplay Gabrul."

A few hours later we swept the sleeping town like a cyclone — Billy Logan, in character, as the devil with a pitchfork, leading.

We reached our rooms about three o'clock A.M., pretty well tired. As Billy flung open his door, there sat Isrul fast asleep in his arm-chair, with the empty bottle beside him, and his old basket between his feet well filled with Billy's effects. He had been overtaken in the very act. "Get up here! I'm going to kill you and bury you," Billy shouted. He seized him by the collar and pulled him out of the chair. As he let him go, Isrul fell in a drunken heap on the floor. Billy disappeared, with two or three fellows, and in a little while came back with a bucket of paint and the finest coffin from Little Dole's, the undertaker's, shop. The old Doctor and Little Dole both declared next day that it was burglary; but I think they took an extreme view of it. Little Dole had lost his front door and his best coffin, and "the old Doctress," as we profanely called the Doctor's wife, was exciting him about the rape of her greenhouse. Anyhow, Billy got the coffin, and old Isrul, his face painted a livid blue, and his chin tied up like a corpse's with one of Billy's handkerchiefs, and every flower from the old Doctress's greenhouse on his breast, was borne out. The hall used as a chapel was forcibly entered, and "the corpse" was borne in. Billy officiated, his devil's head poking up over the Doctor's gown. He had the Doctor's very voice. Perhaps it was the Doctor's voice which startled "the corpse," but anyhow he opened his eyes. He got ashier under his coat of paint as he fixed his gaze on Billy's horns. The devil raised his fork.

"Now at last we have him in torment. What shall we do with him?" he asked, in a terrific voice.

"Damn him!" came from two hundred throats.

"Light the fire," he said. He turned towards the victim and brandished his pitchfork. "How many hen-roosts have you robbed?" he asked.

Isrul's jaw worked. His eyes were popping out of his head. "M-m-marse Satan, y-y-you ain' gwine back befo' de war, is you?" he asked.

"Since."

"I-I don' know, m-master; not but three, I b'lieve."

He was evidently in doubt.

"He has lied; record it. Add three hundred years for each one he left out."

There was an awful addition with sticks on the floor at the head of the coffin. A hundred throats responded, "It is recorded." Isrul groaned.

"How often have you been drunk?"

"I-I-I don' know, master; I done forgit," he said, seeking safety in oblivion.

"Add two hundred years."

It was added on the floor.

"How often have you stolen from the college students, particularly from that pious, virtuous, upright, and righteous gentleman, Billy Logan?"

"I-I—'bout a million times," faltered Isrul.

There was a groan on all sides.

"He has told one truth; take off two minutes. Heat the fire, and set the big middle kettle to boiling."

A red calcium-light suddenly lit up the scene, turning the devil's head and flowing robe a fiery red. He brandished his pitchfork and advanced. With a yell, Isrul sprang from the coffin. The devil caught him, and they clinched; and the two rolled around together in a medley of coffin, legs, chairs, pitchforks, and devil's horns, Isrul yelling and fighting for salvation, the devil tangled up in the Doctor's gown, which was being torn to shreds, shouting to us to help him. Suddenly Isrul dealt him a tremendous blow, broke loose, and with one bound sprang crashing through the nearest window, taking the sash with him, and Billy, with his gown in tatters and his mask torn off, scrambled breathless to his feet. We saw him start to speak, then look towards the door. A change came over his face, and with a shout of "The Doctor!" he swept the lamp from the table and followed Isrul through the shattered window—followed by the rest of us, pell-mell.

The attendance at chapel next morning was better than it had been before in years. Every student showed up. Billy was the demurest of the congregation, sat well forward, but kept in the shadow of a pillar to hide an ugly bruise over the eye, and sang devoutly. The coffin had been removed, but there was no need of a coffin to make the occasion solemn. Little Dole sat on the front bench, and the Doctor's face wore a look of doom. I believe every man of the three hundred stopped breathing. I know I did. He said a great outrage had been committed (Little Dole groaned), and that the faculty had met and determined to inflict the severest punishment in their power —expulsion. "We shall expel every one concerned in its perpetration. The town authorities will probably follow it up with a prosecution." (Little Dole grunted.) The Doctor paused. You could put your hand out and feel the silence. "—As soon as the perpetrators are discovered," he added. A hundred men drew long breaths.

It was late in the afternoon when we saw an old lame darky hobbling across the lawn with a stick. His mother would hardly have recognized him. His eye was apparently bunged up, his head was plastered over with court-plaster like a map, his arm was in a sling, and he was so lame he could scarcely hobble; but he was evidently not entirely blind, for he was making straight for the Doctor's office. He was nearly there. Billy gazed at him intently, and suddenly cut out of the door, we after him. It was Isrul. He had actually reached the door and raised his hand to knock when Billy got to him.

"Wait. Come here; I want to speak to you," he said to him, in a breathless undertone, beckoning him away from the door.

"Who dat?" asked Isrul, lifting his head and peering at him out of his bunged-up eye, as if he could not see him. "Who dat? I cyarn see you. Dat Billy Logan done put my eye out."

"No, he hasn't. How do you know he did it?" said Billy, persuasively. "Come this way a minute; I want to talk to you about it."

"Yes, he did. I got he hankcher wid he name on it. I know he do it. I cyarn heah what you say. Talk louder; he done stop up my ear." He put his hand up to his ear as if to try and hear him.

The Doctor was moving within. Billy, with a look of desperation at the door, caught hold of him. "Come here, Uncle Isrul," he said, seductively.

"Ough!" cried Isrul. "Umh! Dat boy done breck my arm. He done ruin me for life." He raised his voice.

"No, he didn't. Don't talk so loud, please, sir," expostulated Billy, with a glance at the door. "If you come this way I'll talk to you about it."

"I don' want to talk to you. I want to talk to de Doctor. Who is you? You ain' de Doctor, is you? I cyarn see you." He raised his head again as if to try and see his interlocutor, groaned with pain, and then turned to the door and caught the knocker.

"Come here. I'll pay you, Uncle Isrul."

Isrul paused. "How much you gwine pay me?"

"I'll pay you well. Come here; come on." Billy's voice was never so enticing.

"I cyarn walk. Dat boy done breck my leg."

"I'll help you; I'll carry you. Come on," and he took the old fellow and helped him hobble along, almost carrying him to his room. "Come in." He flung the door open. But Isrul sank down at the step with a groan, exhausted. Billy offered him five dollars not to tell. He was obdurate. At last Billy in despair asked him what he would hold his tongue for. He reflected, then turned and glanced around inside the room through his almost closed eyes. "Gim me dat new suit o' clo'es." Billy called him by a bad name.

Isrul pulled himself up with a groan, and

started for the Doctor's. Just as he reached the door, Billy rushed after him. His education, his future, his sweetheart, hung on the issue. Breathing threatenings and slaughter, he went to get the clothes. Isrul examined them critically, and poked them into his basket.

"Whar de beaver?" he asked in surprise, looking around as if he expected to see that article lying beside the basket.

It was not in the contract, explained Billy; but to no purpose.

"Oh yes, it was," said Isrul. "Suit o' clo'es ain' nuttin' 'dout de beaver. You kin teck 'em back. I want to see de Doctor anyways."

He took the clothes out, and rose painfully.

The beaver was brought, and having put it carefully into his basket on top of the clothes, and surrendered the handkerchief, Isrul rose.

"Good-evenin', Marse Satan," he said. "I'll have de music dyah in time to-night;" and he hobbled off.

Billy spent the afternoon having the rents made the night before in his old black coat sewed up, so that he could wear it to the ball. He was a little late in arriving.

"'GOOD EVE'NIN', MARSE SATAN'"

As he led Miss Mabel up the floor to the head of the room, his eyes fell on the players. Well out in front of them sat Isrul, as well as he ever was in his life, without a scratch on him, and decked out in Billy's new suit, and with his beaver cocked on his woolly head. He waited till Billy reached his place, then threw his head back, and took a long look at him, with his eyes nearly closed, as if trying to see him, caught his eye, and bowed low to him. " Good-evenin', Marse Satan," he said, lifted his elbow, and, with a triumphant wag of his head, shouted, " S'lute your pardners," and began to " outplay Gabrul."

THE TRUE STORY OF THE SURRENDER OF THE MARQUIS CORNWALLIS

I HAD the honor done me once to be appointed Provisional Secretary and Treasurer of the State Chapter of the Society of the Sons of the Revolution, or of the American Revolution; I never could remember which. (To this unhappy fault of memory I owed my early removal from the responsible and remunerative office; for the offspring of the two Revolutions were like the first pair of brothers, not wholly in unity.) In the discharge of this office I became acquainted with a good deal of history which has satisfied me that the commonly received versions are far from accurate. Among the true accounts which I thus received is the following story of the surrender of the Marquis Cornwallis, which was related to me by an eye-witness, and is, therefore, of course, true.

I was seated one day in my office, when there came a tap at my door. It differed essentially from either the deferential tap of a client, or the more imperious rap of the creature who carries around a packet of long, narrow invitations to settle, the acceptance of which keeps a man poor. This knock was light and tentative, and yet had in it a certain assertion.

"Come in," I called.

It was repeated. I knew then that it was not the gentleman of the narrow and inconvenient invitations. He never waits to be invited twice. Sometimes he comes even when a response is withheld. I called more boldly, "Come in."

The door opened slowly, and a person entered—a little, old, dried-up-looking individual with a little, old, dried-up black face, surmounted by a little, old, dried-up black beaver. The white corners of two little eyes, or of what from their geographical position I supposed were eyes, were visible. The visitor, with his back to me, closed the door without the slightest sound, as carefully as if a creak would have blown the house down. Then he turned and faced me.

"Well?" I said. "What is it?"

"Sarvent, suh. Is dis de place whar you gits you' money?"

"No, it is not," I said, feeling that I was safe within the bounds of truth this far.

"'Tain't?" He reflected a little while. "Dis de place dee tole me was de place." He gazed all around curiously.

"Who told you?" I asked.

"Dee. Who is you? Is you de American Rebelution?" His little eyes were on me scrutinizingly.

"Well, I believe I am; but I am not sure," I said.

"Well, you's de one." He looked relieved. "I is de son of de Rebelution."

This cast some doubt on my identity.

"You are the son of which one?" I asked, having learned to be discreet.

"Of bofe," he said. "I wuz right dyah at de time—in little York. I seed it all."

"You saw it? What?"

"Generul Wash'n't'n's surrender. I seed it. I seed it when he come a-gallinupin' up on he big iron-gray haws, an' I see de Markiss Cornwallis, too. I see 'em bofe."

I began to be interested.

"I IS DE SON OF DE AMERICAN REBELUTION"

"You saw it all?" I asked. "Well, tell me about it."

"Den you gwine gi' me my money?"

"Yes, if it is not too much."

"Well, I'll tell you," he said. "You see 'twuz dis a-way. I wuz born right dyah in little York. My mammy she wuz de nuss for ole missis chillern, an' I wuz—"

"Wait; how old are you?" I asked.

"I don' know how ole I is. I so ole I done forgit. I know I is over a hunderd. I know I is, 'cuz I wuz twelve year ole when my mammy die, an' she die when she had nuss ole missis lars gal, jes after de holidays, de littles' one o' all, an' I know she wuz ol'er 'n ole missis. I know I is over a hunderd. I reckon maybe I is two hunderd—maybe I is."

This was convincing, so I said, "Go on. You know all about it."

"Oh, yes, suh, I knows all about it. Hi! how I gwine help it? Warn't I right dyah! seein' of it fum de top of de ole Father Aberham apple-tree in ole marster gyardin? Markiss Cornwallis he had done been dyah for I don' know how long, jes a-bossin' it 'roun', eatin' off o' ole marster bes' chany an' silver whar Nat rub up, an' chawin' tobacker, an' orderin' roun' jes big as ole marster. An' he use' to strut roun' dyah, an' war he beaver hat an' he swo'd, an' set on de front poach, an' drink he julep jes like he own all de niggers fum Pigeon Quarter spang to Williamsbu'g. An' he say ef Gen'l Wash'n'n jes dyah to set he foot dyah he'd teck de hide off him, he say. An' one day, jes after dinner, he wuz settin' on de poach a-smokin' he cigar, an' come a nigger on a mule wid a note, an' he look at it, an' squint he eye up dis a-way, an' say, 'Heah he now.' An' de urrs say, 'Who?' An' he say, 'Dat feller, Gen'l Wash'n'n.' An' de say, 'He want me to s'render.' An' dee all laugh. An' he say, 'You go back, an' tell him I say to come on, an' ef he come I'll teck de hide off'n him,' he say, 'an' I'll whup him wid one han' 'hine my back,' he say. 'Talk 'bout s'render!' he say. An' he sont de nigger back, an' holler for he haws an' he swo'd. An' fus' thing you know, heah come Gen'l Wash'n'n a-ridin' on a big iron-gray, a gol' pum'l to he saddle, an' a silver bit to he bridle long as you' arm, an' a gol' cyurb to it big as log-chain, an' a swo'd by he side long as a fence-rail. An' as he come ridin' up he say, ' Did'n' I tole you to s'render?' he say. ' You don' s'render, don' you ?' he say. An' Markiss Cornwallis soon as he see him he wuz so skeert he ain' know what to do. He jes turn white as you' shut, an' he ain' wait ner nuttin' ; he jes took out hard as he could stave it. An' Gen'l Wash'n'n he teck out after him, an' he hollers, ' Stop! s'render!' says he. An' he say, ' I ain' gwine s'render,' says he. An' he wuz a-ketchin' up wid him; an' Markiss Cornwallis he teck out roun' a apple-tree — a gre't big apple-tree — a Father Aberham apple-tree. An' Gen'l Wash'n'n he teck out right after him, an' dyah dee hed it! Well, suh, you nuver see san' fly so in you' life. Fus' Markiss Cornwallis, an' den Gen'l Wash'n'n. Markiss Cornwallis he wuz ridin' of a little sorrel pacin' myah, an' she wuz jes a-movin' ; her legs look like guinea-hen's. Gen'l Wash'n'n he wuz ridin' of a big iron-gray haws, an' he wuz gwine like elephant. De myah war'n' nowhar. An' ev'y now an' den Gen'l Wash'n'n he hollers out an' say, 'S'render!' an' Markiss Cornwallis he say, ' I ain' gwine s'render,' says he, an' he wuz jes a-flyin'. An' pres'n'y Gen'l Wash'n'n he come up wid him—even—so, an' he draws he swo'd, an' Markiss Cornwallis he holler out an' say, 'I s'renders,' says he. But 'tain' no use to say 's'render' den. Gen'l Wash'n'n he done git he blood up, an' he say, 'Oh yes,' he say. 'Who dat you gwine teck de hide off'n him?' he say, an' he jes drawed he weepin', an' he giv' a swipe, an' he cut he head right clean off, he did. Yes, suh; he done dat thing, 'cuz I seed him.—Whar wuz I? I wuz right up in de apple-tree.—What did I do? I jes slip' down out'n de tree an' hol' Gen'l Wash'n'n haws for him while he wuz cuttin' he head off; an' when he git thoo, he say, 'Felix, how's de Cun'l an' de ladies an' de fambly?' an' he wipes he swo'd, an' put 't back in de scabbard, an' when he git ready to mount, he gi' me two an' threepence, an' says he, 'Felix, a gent'man nuver gies less 'n dat to a servant,' says he.—Suh?

"Well, suh, anything you choose. You is a gent'man, I see; an' Gen'l Wash'n'n he say a gent'man nuver gies a servant less 'n— Thankee, suh; I knowed you wuz a gent'-man."

WHEN LITTLE MORDECAI WAS AT THE BAR

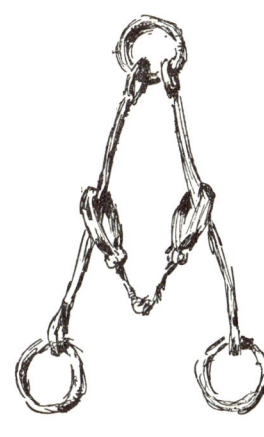

ALL lawyers have a sufficiently good opinion of their profession, but the proudest member of the bar that ever was was Peter Hankins, "Jedge Peter," as he was called. The "jedge" had a prescriptive right to his title. He had filled the position of office-boy, boot-black, book-carrier, body-servant, and toddy-mixer for every lawyer in the circuit for two generations, besides sweeping up the Court-house, filling the inkstands, and being general factotum for the clerk, the sheriff, and the jailer.

He had eventually retired, owing to a change of administration in the Court-house, coupled, on his part, with habitual drunkenness and contemptuous reference to the new régime, and was thereafter compelled to dig potatoes and do odd jobs like any other common hand; but he never regarded his subsequent occupation as any thing at all, and held everything modern in sovereign contempt. He was too proud generally to enter in a private capacity the court-room in which he had once presided officially. It was only on extraordinary occasions, such as murder trials, that he ever relaxed his dignity so far as to enter the precincts once so familiar to him, and he atoned for it when there by carrying his head with an air, and wearing on his face a look, of disdain which would have warranted the judge in sending him to jail for contempt of court. Whatever happened, he was ready with," When me an' Little Mordicai was at de bar, suh."

It was thus that he happened to be present at the trial of the murderer who killed a woman in the lower end of the county, and who, after coming near being hanged by the mob, was saved by Judge Gaston through one of the ablest defences ever known in the State. The jury at first hung for a short time, but the crowd was completely carried away by the judge's masterly speech, and it was at this crisis that Jedge Peter was found busily engaged outside of the court-green, with ostentatious indifference, making a wedge for his hoe-handle. McPheeters went up to him.

"Jedge, fine speech Judge Gaston made, wasn't it?" he asked him.

Jedge Peter turned his hoe around slowly and measured the eye, stuck the wedge a little way in it, and straightened up. " Gashcum! Gashcum!" he said, disdainfully. "What does I know about yo' Jedge Gashcum? I's heered Little Mordicai when I was at de bar."

This was what McPheeters wanted, and he told him of the jury being hung.

"Yes, an' he hung de jury too," declared the jedge, his chin high in the air, and his whole figure expressing his disdain. "Hung de jury, an' hung de cote, an' ev'ybody else, an' hung th'ee good plantations an' two hunderd niggers in his deed of intrust, too, in he breeches-pocket, he did."

McPheeters looked incredulous, and tolled him on. "Who was his client, and what had he done?"

"He client? He had so many clients I

cyarn 'member de one he had dat time, but he had done do some'n sho 'nough! He hadn' killed no little po' one white ooman; he had done kilt th'ee womens—*th'ee* womens! Jes so, 'dout no consideratin' hat all; had jes chop dee haids wide open, an' cut 'em up like you cut up hawgs. Dee fotch him up heah, an' lodge him in jail, and tell me to keep him, an' dat I did! I lock him up dyah in de cell wid log-chain roun' him like a bull; an' de folks wuz so rabid 'bout him I tell de Gov'ner to stan' by me (dee warn' like dem few mens turr night, hollerin' an' drinkin' whiskey aroun'; de whole county wuz out), an' he sont me a comp'ny o' millingtary, an' 'twuz all me an' dee could do together to keep 'em fum him. But we did, an' we hilt him good till de trial come on. Dat wuz a trial as wuz a trial! De whole State wuz dyah. An' de th'ee womens dee went an' hired th'ee la'yers apiece to pussecute him, dat made ten, 'cuz you know dee's al'ays a pussecutin' la'yer fur de State to eternally pussecute, an' dee come heah in dee gigs wid de books an' papers, an' lock de do', an' wouldn' le' nobody come in but me; 'cuz dee hed to insult me, an' I wuz 'bleeged to be dyah, 'cuz I hed done put de log-chain on him. Dem ten wuz 'bleeged to be dyah, 'cuz de prisoner he wuz a pleader; he wouldn' hev no la'yer roun' heah for him; he hed done sont all de way down fur Little Mordicai."

"Little Mordicai?" said McPheeters, inquiringly.

"Yes, Little Mordicai! Little Mordicai warn' no Gashcum; he wuz a la'yer. Dee wuz giants in dem days. He come in a gig wid his portmantia behin' him, an' he tell me to teck it off an' cyah 't to he room, an' bresh he boots, an' he wash, an' put on he ruffled shut, an' teck he snuff-box, an' tell me to come on— an' he went to de jail, an' I open de do', an' he teck out he snuff-box, an' he ax me whar 'dat dam scoundrel' wuz, an' I le' him in, an' he tole me to hol' de do', an' he walk in an' look at him settin' dyah on he bed with my log-chain on him—he look at him tell he look like he dwindlin' up. An' he say presney, 'Is you Little Mordicai?' An' he say, 'Yes; an' I big Mordicai too,' he say. An' he say, 'I warn' you to defen' me,' he say. An' Little Mordicai he say, 'How much does you think your dam neck is wuth?' he say. An' he say, 'I will give you a thousan' dollars; I is a po' man,' he say. An' Little Mordicai he teck a pinch o' snuff, dis away, an' he say, 'Dem wuz po' womens too,' he say; 'an' you is got th'ee plantations on de Roanoke an' two hunderd niggers,' he say. An' he say, 'I will give you two thousan' dollars,' he say. An' Little Mordicai he teck up a pinch o' snuff, dis away, an' he pitch it away dat away, an' he say, 'Two thousan' dollars ain' wuff dat,' he say. 'I'll see you' dam neck breck befo' I will open my mouf for less 'n ten thousan' dollars,' he say, 'on a deed o' intrust,' he say; 'an' you will fry in hell too, a thousan' years,' he say. An' he shiver like a p'inter-dog, jes so, an' he say, 'I will do it.' An' Little Mordicai retch he han' in he pocket, an' pull de deed o' intrust out he pocket wid de whereas an' de hereditaments aforesaid, an' teck a pen an' ink out he weskit pocket, whar he cyared 'em reg'lar, an' meck him sign it right dyah, an' swar to it wid de hereditaments aforesaid, 'cuz he know he wuz 'bleeged to had him, settin' dyah wid de chain roun' him, an' he hed done fotch de deed o' intrust wid him, wid all de whereas

an' de plantations an' niggers an' de hereditaments aforesaid, an' he put he name to it, an'
kiss de book right dyah befo' him, whar he
cyared aroun' fur dem pupposes as aforesaid.
An' Little Mordicai put de deed o' intrust in
he pocket an' button it up, an' nuver say anurr
word to him, jes tu'n an' went back to supper,
an' set down wid de jedge an' all, an' tole 'em
to lef' de man in jail. An' dat night he ain'
sleep none, he bu'n seben candles readin' o' he
deed o' intrust wid de whereas an' de hereditaments aforesaid. An' de nex' day he went
'way; an' de cote meet, an' dee lef' de man in
jail wid de log-chain on him, an' meet agin an'
lef' him dyah, an' meet agin, an' den de Gran'
Jury redite him. An' when Little Mordicai
come dat time, he wuz a-ridin' of a fine black
thery-bred myah wid two white foots, an'
laigs jes keen as blacksnakes, an' he had injy-
rubber shoes on her; an' when de cote meet
dat mornin' he tole me to tie her dyah at de
fence jes outside de cote-yard gate. An' when
de trial camed on de millingtary wuz dyah:
dee hed de man dyah in de Cote-house; an' de
ten la'yers whar de th'ee womens he kilt done
hire to wrassle wid Little Mordicai an' to pus-

secute him, an' de commonwealth's attorney whar eternally pussecutes; dee hed a steer-cart load o' books dyah dee meck me spread out on de bar befo' 'em; I strain my back dee wuz so many; I 'ain' git over it yit (dat's de way I happen to be in de Cote-house to-day; hit hut me so, I wuz tryin' to res' it; I ain' keerin' nuttin' 'bout dis heah little Gashcum jestice trials); dee hed a whole fo'-hoss waggin-load o' books spread out on de bar, an' dee riz an' made dee speeches, an' tell de jedge 'bout de womens de murderer hed done kill, an' ax Little Mordicai is he ready, an' sot down, an' Little Mordicai riz. He didn' had but one book, jes byah one book, de curisomes'-lookin' book you ever see; 'twarn' boun' like turr books; de back wuz sort o' comicle like it hed been buried; an' he open it slow, sort o' so, an' he face wuz sort o' curisome-lookin', an' he tell 'em to teck de chains off'n de prisoner, dat de internal consicution didn' 'low no prisoner to wyar chains in cote; an' dat dee done; an' de crowd wuz so thick roun' you couldn' breathe; an' de millingtary dee wuz dyah to stan' by me; an' Little Mordicai he teck pinch o' snuff, sort o' so, an' look roun' an' bresh he shut ruffle, sort o' so, an' bow to ev'ybody. Den he begin.

"He pay he bespects to all de pussecutin' gent'mens, an' to de cote, an' to all on us gent'mens on de bar, an' to de crowd an' de millingtary, an' den he riz a pint, jes a pint; he hed a barrel he could 'a' riz, but a pint wuz 'nough fur him; an' he tuck up de book, de curisome-lookin' book, an' riz a pint, an' he read, an' 'twuz so larnèd dee couldn' nobody onderstan' him; dee say 'twuz dead languidge, an' de book hed been buried a hunderd thousan' year, an' he riz de pint, jes one pint, like I say, an' dat wuz—dat wuz dat dee couldn' hang de man, an' dee couldn' even try him; dat wuz he pint. An' talk about hung jury! He hang de jury, an' he hang de jedge, an' he hang de folks all roun' him, dee couldn' budge; dee jes set dyah right still, jes like nail druv in plank, like dee wuz tricked. An' de jedge say, ' Las' cote, an' de cote 'fo' dat, an' de cote 'fo' dat. Well, dam me ef 'tain' so!' An' dee all set right still an' speechless, an' jes Little Mordicai stan'in' up, smilin' an' curisome-lookin', an' de murderer settin' by him, white an' trimblin'; an' Little Mordicai he turned an' whisper a word, jes a word, to de man, an' he riz an' walk out o' de Cote-house right easy, like he wuz tiptoein' not to wake 'em up, an' made a dart for de cote-green gate, an' flung heself on de back o' de black myah, an' headed her down de road jes as de crowd in de Cote-house breck fum onder de spell o' Little Mordicai's pint, an' po'ed roarin' out o' de Cote-house arter him. Dee 'd 'a' limbered him ef dee could 'a' got him; but shuh! dat wuz Little Mordicai's myah wid de blacksnake laigs. De devil hed done brecked her; she riz up off de groun' an' flew jes like a bud. She didn' meck a piece o' track, didn' lef' nuttin' but a cloud o' dust, an' nurr she nor dat man ever been seed sence.

"An' Little Mordicai he come out de Cote-house smilin', teckin' snuff, wid he arm roun' de pussecutin' 'torney's neck, an' he went an' live' on he th'ee plantations wid de deed o' intrust an' de whereas an' de two hunderd niggers an' de hereditaments aforesaid. Dat's what he done!

"Gashcum! Don' talk to me 'bout your Gashcum! He couldn' 'a' open he mouf in de Cote-house when me an' Little Mordicai wuz at de bar!"

"'HE RIZ JES' A P'INT, JES' ONE P'INT'"

CHARLIE WHITTLER'S CHRISTMAS PARTY

I MET them just after I came to town to practise law. They were engaged in what they termed " journalism." Philologically the term was appropriate, for they lived literally from day to day. They could have secured positions which would have maintained them —at least, Henry could, for he was a man of parts, and has made his mark since in another profession — but what did they want with positions? They were " journalists," and were bound to be famous or die. I suppose that together they made sixty dollars a month— some months — and spent a hundred, or as much more as they could.

" When we make ten dollars we live on it," said Henry.

" When we make fifty dollars we give a ball," said Charlie.

But they were rich—two of the richest men

I ever knew. Certainly Charlie was. He already owned one of the great newspapers, which he was going to make eclipse the Thunderer. He only had not got possession of it yet. They lived in a brownstone palace; the little back third-story room at Mrs. McDuffy's was only temporary quarters which they occupied for convenience. It was there that they invited me the day before Christmas, "to open the festivities with eggnog and a little supper."

"Don't ring or knock; just walk right up to the third floor," said Charlie. "We have our apartments in the third story for the light and air. Nothing like pure air for pure reasoning, and clear light for clearness of expression."

He went off talking about "the beauties of nature" to be studied from his windows, by which he must have meant the sky, and the English sparrows which built in the eaves. He may have detected me looking at his old patent-leather pumps, once the pride of his college days, now worn into holes; his threadbare coat, and his faded hat; for he said, suddenly,

"My dear boy, I will give you a hint in domestic economy: always wear your shabbiest clothes the day before a ball; they will make your others look new next day."

When I arrived, the following evening, I disobeyed Charlie's injunction. I did not ring, for a good reason. The bell had long since disappeared: carried off, Charlie declared later, by Henry in a wild attempt to rival Samson one Saturday night when Mrs. McDuffy had locked the door on him.

"I was trying to arouse Mrs. McDuffy," said Henry.

"You aroused her," said Charlie. "If it had not been for my presence of mind, she would have turned us out into the street."

"If it had not been for your presence of body, I would have turned her out," said Henry.

Charlie shook his head mournfully.

"You have no idea what a time I have keeping the peace," he said. "I have told Mrs. McDuffy lies enough on his account to take a thousand years of purgatory."

"And enough on your own account to take two thousand," said Henry.

But I am anticipating. This was told me after I got up to the apartments. When I arrived at the house, not liking the look of the dark passage and narrow stairs shown by the little smoky lamp in the window, I knocked — knocked not once, but twenty times, without the slightest result. The twenty-first time, however, was a thunderer. It created a stir somewhere below; for from the basement I heard a voice which told that Mrs. McDuffy was "aroused."

"An' who is that thryin' to break the door down now?" she shouted as she climbed the stairs. I prepared for the worst; but it was worse even than I had expected. She was a stout and grizzled Irishwoman, whose absent eye was said by Charlie to have been lost in a conflict with the lamented McDuffy, who had, however, come off from the mêlée worse than his spouse, as he had disappeared and had never been heard from again, a fact which gave Henry's designation of him as "the departed" a peculiarly appropriate significance.

"An' is it breakin' the door down intoirly ye're afther?" she asked as she advanced, war in her voice and in her garments. She was evidently just out of the kitchen, as I discovered with more senses than that which noted the yellow cake-dough on her brawny arms. My civil answer mollified her somewhat; but on my asking if my friends lived there, she burst out again: " Live here, is it ? Yis, an' that they do, an' Bridget McDuffy is the wan as knas it, too. An' lives on the fat of the lan', they do; an' gits it out of may, they do, too; may a poor widder, or as good as wan, an' not a tin-cint pace o' their money has I sane for three months; an' they pramisin' to pay me every wake, an' a-drinkin' an' a-guzzlin' themselves up-stairs as full as St. Pathrick's well, an' borryin' all o' me best glasses an' sphoons, an' niver the manners to say wanst to may, 'Mrs. McDuffy, will ye walk in an' wet ye' whistle ?' "

This and much more, till I reached the third floor, where I announced myself by falling up three steps. I found Charlie in his shirt sleeves, and with the seat of his breeches rather out, but with a shiny new beaver on the back of his head, presiding over a large bowl of egg-nog made in the wash-basin, while Henry was preparing something over a not very large fire. One or two other fellows were already assembled, and, in default of chairs, were lying on the bed, and were being entertained by reminiscences of Mrs. McDuffy, evidently called forth by the sound of her voice below.

"So Cerberus caught you?" said Henry as I entered. "By Jove! when I heard you tumble, I thought she was flinging you down the steps."

"Why, Henry!" said Charlie, reproachfully. Then to us: "She really has a beautiful temper. She is a little ruffled this evening, owing to the way Henry approached her on a small domestic matter." He stirred in the whiskey.

"Approached her!" said Henry. "If you had bought the things instead of buying that beaver to put on your empty head, I should not have had to go to her. What do you fellows think of my giving him the money to get up the ball, and his spending it all in a beaver hat and silk handkerchiefs!"

Charlie protested that a beaver hat and silk handkerchiefs were the first necessity for a gentleman who was going to give a supper to an Irish lord on Christmas Eve. "Besides, didn't I get the eggs and whiskey?" he asked.

"Yes; but where's the supper?" asked Henry.

"I bet you this hat against your best pair of breeches I get it yet," said Charlie.

"Done," said Henry. "I will wear that hat to church to-morrow."

"I told her we were going to have an Irish lord to sup with us," said Charlie, "and I would have got everything all right if Henry had not spoilt it. Lord McCarthy, of Castle McCarthy, County Kerry, Ireland — wasn't that the name I gave?" He addressed Henry. "Mrs. McDuffy came from County Kerry; but rather young. Some years ago, I may observe."

"Well, you had better go and get some coal from her; for this fire is going out, I may observe," said Henry, straightening up.

"Where are the slats?" asked Charlie. "Aren't there still four left?"

"Yes; but there are no more slats to spare. The bed feels like a gridiron now."

"Better men than you have lain on a gridiron," said Charlie. "What a sybarite you are!" He stirred in more whiskey. "Why not sleep on the floor? That is the natural place to sleep, anyhow."

"No, I'll be hanged if I do," said Henry.

"And I suppose we could not spare another

chair?" He gazed over at Henry doubtfully; but Henry shook his head positively.

"Why, then you must go down-stairs and get it," he said, cheerfully.

"Down-stairs! Where? We haven't any coal down-stairs."

"We have not! Why, of course we have! Do you suppose we are going to let an old Irishwoman sleep with her coal-cellar literally bulging with coal whilst we have no fire?— entertaining a real live Irish lord too!"

"Suppose we borrow some from Pestler," suggested Henry. Pestler was the little apothecary next door.

But Charlie was shocked. "Borrow of a demned petty tradesman, and the night before Christmas, too!" he exclaimed. "Where is your pride? Besides, I borrowed some from him last week. Go down and get some coal."

But Henry was obdurate. He told him to go and get it himself; which Charlie finally proceeded to do.

"What are you going to bring it up in?" asked Henry.

"Why, this," said Charlie, stripping the pillow-case from the only pillow left with that article on it. He disappeared down the stairs, and a little later we heard a smash as of a door breaking, and a minute afterwards we heard him coming hastily back up the steps, evidently with a burden on his back. Suddenly, there was another sound: the voice of Mrs. McDuffy broke on the air.

"An' where is he? the thievin', burglin' villain! Let me get at him. I'll fix him. Breakin' down me house an' robbin' me under me very eyes!" She came stamping up the stairs. Charlie quickened his steps, but she was evidently gaining on him. Suddenly, there was the most tremendous crash. The pillow-case had parted in the middle, and the whole load rolled down the steps, nearly carrying Mrs. McDuffy with it. Charlie bounded into the room with a single large lump in his hand, and with the upper half of the slip, which he had saved.

"Don't lock the door, Henry; Mrs. McDuffy will be up directly to call on us," he said, his face glowing with excitement, as Henry sprang to the door. Mrs. McDuffy was, indeed, already there. The next instant she nearly knocked the door from its hinges. She evidently believed it locked. Charlie flung it wide open, and stood full in it.

"Why, is that you, Mrs. McDuffy?" he asked, in a tone of pleased surprise, holding out his yet grimy hand.

"Yis, an' yis, an' yis, it is Mrs. McDuffy, an' if ye don't kna' her, I mane to make ye kna' her," panted the enraged landlady, her fists clenched and her arms akimbo. She paused for breath. It was Charlie's opportunity.

"Know you! Why, of course, I know you, Mrs. McDuffy," said he, in the blandest of tones. "I have got a drop of the Irish in me meself" (which was true if he was talking about whiskey). "Me mither was Irish, ye kna'" (dropping into the brogue). "Her father was a Doherty, from County Kerry, an' I never forgets the pretty Irish face wanst I says it. I was thinkin' of coomin' down to ask ye if ye would not faiver us by coomin' up an' joinin' us. Sure I was just sayin' to me friend here, if ye want to say the prettiest Irishwoman this side of the say, it's down-stairs she is, says I, an' maybe we kin git her to come up, says I. An' I'll joust stale down, says I, an' break

"'I HAVE GOT A DROP OF THE IRISH IN ME, MESELF'"

into her coal-box, says I, an' fling a pace or two down the steps, says I, an' that will fetch her up, says I, to say what the divil is the mather av it, says I, an' ye kin say how pretty she is yourself, says I."

Mrs. McDuffy took down her arms, and told him to "git away wid his Irish blarney—not that wanst she had not had her looks as well as the best of them before so much throuble came upon her."

"Throuble, is it? An' throuble indade you have had, Mrs. McDuffy," said Charlie; "but it hasn't touched yer looks. Sure it's yer own darther folks takes you for any time. Why, me friend here was just sayin' to me: 'Who is that likely Irish leddy that let me in the door down-stairs? An' is she a girl or is she married?' says he. 'An' if she's married, is she a widow?' says he. An' I says to him: 'If she was a widow, do ye think she'd be so long,' says I, 'an' me in the house too?' says I. But coom in. I'd like to inthroduce ye to me friend Lord McCarthy, av Castle McCarthy, County Kerry, Ireland. Ye knows all about the McCarthys, I knows, Mrs. McDuffy. You was a Doherty; an' 'Toim was,' says my mither to me wanst—' toim was, Charlie, me boy, when the Dohertys could muster five hundred shillalahs in Kerry.' "

This was too much for Mrs. McDuffy. She came in smiling and blushing; and an hour later, at a table which she had spread with her own hands, and loaded from her own kitchen, her health was proposed by Henry, and was drunk vociferously by all; and Charlie, dressed in Henry's best breeches, responded in the best Irish speech I ever heard.

HOW RELIUS "BOSSED THE RANCH"

RELIUS and I were friends in our bachelor days. He had been in the army, and I naturally looked up to him. He had an idea that he was an austere man, and was fond of referring to his severity. He used to say, "I always boss the ranch." He had been a brave soldier, and I had no reason to doubt his courage on any point. His was one of those natures whose freshness is preserved by its own quality, and though past middle life, he was a man about town, a toast with every one, and had a reputation for coolness if not for anything more. He used to foster the idea with me that he was impudent to women. I never knew that it rendered him unpopular with them. "They like it, sir," he used to say. "All women are slaves, and need a master."

This was his condition when we went to live in the second floor of Mrs. Trouville's little house. Mrs. Trouville had been a friend of his in his youth, when she was in good circumstances, before the war. She was now a sorrowful little widow, slim, refined, and delicate, with the remains of her beauty not yet faded, and with a look in her face and a tone in her voice which were pathetic. I know now that Relius went to live there because she was so poor, though the reason he assigned to me for our move was that Patsy, with whom he made the arrangement, satisfied him that the rooms were the best in town, and that we could not do so well anywhere else. Patsy was Mrs. Trouville's maid, and, I believe, her cook also, though of this I was never sure. She was small, thin, elderly, ladylike, of a dark, walnut brown, and as near a copy of Mrs. Trouville as she could make herself. She moved with a tread as soft as a black cat's, spoke in a tone as low as a whisper, and wore an old black silk dress of Mrs. Trouville's that had been turned more than once. In fact, she copied Mrs. Trouville as faithfully as she served her.

I observed shortly after we moved in that

Patsy treated Relius and me differently. Mrs. Trouville treated us with entire impartiality, being equally kind to both of us, and watchful for our comfort; but Patsy's manner was not the same to us. She brought Relius hot water in the morning, looked after his linen, put his shirt-buttons into his dress-shirts, and placed pillow-shams on his pillows; whilst I shaved cold when I could not wait for Relius's can; looked after my own shirts, and did without pillow-shams. At table she would say to Relius, "More waffles, Mr. Relius?" or, "Another cup of coffee, Mr. Relius?" in a tone hardly above a whisper, but full of quiet interest. I mentioned this to Relius, but he scouted the idea, and declared that I was of an envious nature. If there was a difference, he said it was because he treated Patsy with more severity than I did. "You must hold a woman up to her duty, sir," he said. "You must boss the ranch."

This sedulous care extended. Patsy came to exercise a certain supervision over Relius. She saw that he had on his overshoes in snowy weather, or she, at least, placed them out for him with a constancy which could not be unnoticed. She never said anything: she only looked. Relius gradually became careful how he omitted acting on these unmistakable suggestions. She took to sitting up for him if she knew he was out, just as she did for Mrs. Trouville. Once or twice, on very inclement evenings, he actually, in view of Patsy's silent presence, gave up the idea of going out. He gradually took to dressing very quickly, and slipping out very quietly, in a way that I could not understand, till once I thought I heard him, in answer to a question from Patsy in the hall, tell her that he was not going out, and afterwards found him dressing. I taxed him with it, but he assured me that I was mistaken, which I was willing to admit. At any rate, he slipped out of the house hurriedly, whilst I went out at my leisure; indeed, more slowly than I wished, because I could not find my pet shirt-studs, and had to put up with a broken set. As I passed Patsy on the steps, I told her I wanted her to hunt for the buttons. She made no reply, as usual. We came home together, Relius and I, after a very jolly evening, where Relius had been the life of the party; and he, with his usual considerateness, cautioned me against making any noise, and tripped hastily up the stairs, giving a single glance down over the banisters into the darkness below.

A day or two afterwards he asked me with much concern what in the world I had said to Patsy. I could remember nothing. He said Mrs. Trouville had told him that I had said something to Patsy which had deeply offended her; that Patsy had never before been so spoken to, and that her honesty was above question. I recalled the matter of the shirt-studs, and said I had never dreamed of accusing her of stealing them, and that I would tell her so. He said no; that he thought he had better settle it, which he would do with Mrs. Trouville, and that anyhow it was just as well to keep her up to her duty. I let him do as he pleased.

A short time after this I came home one night and found Relius dressing for a ball. He was nearly dressed, and was rummaging in a drawer, raking the things angrily backwards and forwards, and using very strong language about "that little fool nigger" who would not let things stay where he put them. Finally he asked me to lend him my stud-buttons. I complied, and my generosity moved him to ask me to tell "that fool nigger" after he was gone that he wanted her to find his buttons, and to "let them alone" thereafter. I promptly refused, and asked him if he was afraid to tell her himself.

"Afraid!" he said, with contempt; he only thought that as Patsy was already down on me, it might be better, if we were going to continue to live there, that she should be kept in a good-humor with at least one of us; but as to being "afraid," he would show me that he always bossed his ranch. I heard Patsy let him out, but he said nothing about the buttons.

The next morning I was dressing in my room when I heard Relius talking. I looked in at his door. He was curled up under the cover, and his eyes were fast shut. He was talking, I supposed, in his sleep. I listened. He was saying: "Patsy, I have unfortunately mislaid my stud-buttons. I wish you would hunt for them." The tone was too placid to please him; he began again, on a higher key: "Patsy, my shirt-studs have got mislaid; I want you to hunt for them." This did not satisfy him either, and he began again, quite sternly:

"Patsy, what in the devil have you done with my shirt-studs? Get them for me, and hereafter let them alo—"

Just then the door opened, and Patsy entered, silent as a shadow. Relius shut up like a clam. Patsy moved about, opened the windows, lit the fire, and fixed his water. I watched through the crack of the door. Just as she was going out, Relius yawned, stretched, and opened his eyes as if just waking up.

"Oh, Patsy," he said, in his softest and most insinuating of tones, "if you should happen to come across any shirt-buttons on the floor to-day when you are sweeping, will you please put them up on my bureau for me?"

"Yes, sir," said Patsy, as she passed silently out.

Waiting breathless, until she must be down the stairs, Relius shouted: "Aha! did you hear that? Who says I am afraid of Patsy? Do you see how I boss the ranch?"

When he learned that I had seen, he bought two sets of buttons, and gave me one.

THE PROSECUTION OF MRS. DULLET

I was on a visit to my friend Dave at his mountain home, and was standing one day in the court-yard at Lexby, the county-town, discussing the possibilities of his re-election to the position of commonwealth's attorney, when down the street came, at a long gallop, an old fellow mounted on a thin, ewe-necked, sorrel colt, whose long rusty tail whipped between his legs at every jump. Up to the court-yard gate he clattered, and, dismounting, flung the rein over the post, in utter disregard of the large printed notice posted on it that no horses were to be hitched there. Through the turnstile and up the walk he came swinging.

"I believe that's old Dullet, from Jacksborough," said Dave. "He's a man of influence up there, and dead against me,—always is. I wonder what he wants?"

He had not long to wait; for the old fellow

strode up to a group and said, "Whar's the commonwealth's attorney?"

"I am the man," said Dave. "What can I do for you, Mr. Dullet?"

"I wants you to put my wife in the pen'tentiary," he said.

"What!" exclaimed Dave; then recovered himself. "What do you want that for?"

"She's forged my name, and she's got to go to the pen'tentiary," said he.

"Well, tell me about it," said Dave, seeing the gravity of the situation; and, turning, he led the way into his office, and offered chairs.

"Well, it's this way: My oldest gal, Sairy, is been a-wantin' to marry a feller named Torm Hackle for gwine on two years, and I wouldn't let her."

"Why?" said Dave, in a professional tone, drawing a pen and paper towards him.

"'Cause Torm's on t'other side," said Dullet.

"Oh!" said Dave, writing down something. "Go on."

"Well, I wouldn't let Torm come over on our side. I sont him word ef he did to look out. And Sairy she got kind o' sick and peakèd, and my old woman she wanted me to do it then, and I wouldn't, 'cause I had to sign the dockiment. Then she got kinder worser, and my wife she wanted me to go for the doctor. So day before yistiddy I went down for the doctor, and he said he'd come to-day, and I stayed at Jim Miggins's store all night an' yistiddy a-waitin' for him; an' when I got home last night, my wife she said, 'Whar's the doctor?' And I said, 'He's a-comin'. How's Sairy?' And she said: 'She's done got well. She's got all the doctor she wanted. She's done married Torm Hackle.' 'How did she done it,' says I, 'and I 'ain't signed the license?' says I. 'I signed your name for it,' says she. And I said, 'You has done commit a pen'tentiary offence, and I kin put you in the pen'tentiary for it,' says I. And she bet me a dollar she hadn't and I couldn't; and I says, 'I bet you two dollars I kin and I will,' says I. And now I are gwine to do it. I kin do it, can't I?"

Dave reflected, while the old mountaineer sat still, perfectly passive.

"Well," he said, slowly, "there are not a great many precedents." (The old fellow's

"'YOU HAS DONE COMMIT A PENITENTIARY OFFENCE'"

face hardened.) "But of course," he added, "forgery is a very serious thing, and, ah—" (The old fellow's eye was upon him.) "How long you been married?" he asked.

"Twenty year come next month."

Dave wrote it down.

"Wife always been good wife to you?"

"'Ain' got no fault to find wid her till now, when she forged my name an'—"

"Ever have any trouble with her?"

"Never at all, 'cept, of course, fights like all married folks has."

Dave wrote it down.

"Industrious?"

"Got no fault to find wid her about dat."

"Help you save what you got?"

"Ain't a hard-workin'er, savin'er 'ooman on the mountain."

"How many children she got?"

"Nine—eight livin'. I don't count that one."

"How many dead?"

"Four."

Dave wrote laboriously.

"Wife good to 'em?"

"Jes as good as could be. Nursed 'em faithful."

"Sit up with 'em when they were sick?"

"Never went to bed at all; never took her clothes off."

"Go hard with her?"

"Went mighty hard, specially when Johnny died. He was named after me."

Dave wrote silently.

"Go hard with you?"

"Right sort o' hard."

"Sort o' lonesome after that?"

"Mighty lonesome."

"How old your youngest one now?"

"Gwine on three; that's Billy."

"Fond of his mother?"

"Can't bear her out of his sight."

"Fond of you?"

"Sort of—right smart."

"Say Sairy was your oldest?"

"Yes."

"Thought right smart of her when you didn't have any others, just at first, I reckon?"

"Umh. Might 'a' done; don't remember."

"Wife did, anyhow?"

"Yes; always fool 'bout her. Oldest— see?"

"She was young and fresh then?"

"Yes; likeliest woman on the mountain."

"Bet she was! Used to have good time sitting up to her, going to see her summer evenings, walking through the woods?"

"Yes, sir; did that."

"She thought more of first baby than you. She had more trouble with her than you— when she was a baby, I mean?"

"Oh yes! guess she did."

"Carried her round in her arms, nursed her when she was sick, made her little frocks for her?"

"Yes."

"As she did Johnny's?"

"Yes."

"And does little Billy's?"

"Yes. She's made Billy a little pair of breeches."

"With pockets in them?"

"Yes; two."

Dave laid down his pen, opened the code, and read a little to himself. "Well, I can put her in the penitentiary for you," he said. "'Not less than one nor more than ten years,'" he read.

Dullet sat forward a little.

"How old is your wife?"

"'Bout fifty year."

"I'll draw the indictment. Let me see, the grand jury will meet when? Then the jury?" He was talking to himself, with his eyes turned up to the ceiling. "There might be some of those Hackles on the jury. Umh! that would be bad." (Dullet twisted around in his chair.) "They'd send her on for the full time, though—ten years. That would be good."

Dullet leaned forward. "Are them Hackles obleeged to be on that jury?" he asked.

"No," said Dave; "not at all. Only they may be on there, that's all." He lifted his eyes again to the ceiling. "That might be all the better. They'd of course be pretty rough on her. Ten years. She'd be about sixty when she came out. Umh! They'd have worked her pretty hard—let me see; I suppose they'd put her with the thieves, dress her in stripes, maybe whip her." (Dullet started to give an exclamation, but stopped to listen.) "I suppose little Billy would be sorry at night at first, but he'd get used to it; or he might go down to see her once a

year or so, for a few minutes, in his breeches
—if she lived; he'd miss her some. If she
died, she'd go to Johnny. Well, the Hackles
wouldn't be sorry. Yes, I can do it, I think,"
he said, bringing his eyes down on Dullet's
face, and speaking positively.

Dullet rose with a jump. "Look a-here,
Mr.— Mr.—What's-your-name?" he said.
"I'll just be durned ef any of them damned
Hackles can put my wife in the pen'tentiary;
and ef anybody thinks they kin, let 'em try
it!"

Dave looked at him calmly. "I agree with
you," he said, "and I'll help you."

There was a pause, in which Dullet was
reflecting. Then he asked, "What would
you edvise me to do?"

"I don't advise you to do anything," said
Dave; "but I know what I'd do if I was in
your place."

"What?"

"I'd go home and send for Sairy to come
over to dinner next Sunday, and tell her to
bring that fellow with her—he's more Dullet
now than he is Hackle; and every time my
wife got uppish I'd tell her I could have put

her in the penitentiary for ten years, but I was too good to her to do it."

Dullet reflected, and then said, " I'll do it. What does I owe you?"

"A good deal," said Dave; " but I want you to present it to Mrs. Dullet for me."

" Well—" He walked to the door, paused, and then said, slowly, " Th' nex' time you runs for anything, Jacksborough is a-gwine to vote for you." He went out.

Dave was re-elected.

ONE FROM FOUR

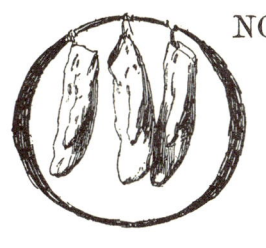

ONCE upon a time there was a lady who was young, beautiful, accomplished, and very rich. She was also very clever. But her most striking characteristic was that she was every atom a woman. She had three lovers, who had been college cronies. She always spoke of them as her "friends." There was a fourth gentleman whom she knew, but by no means so intimately, who was a friend of the other three.

One of the three "friends" was tall, handsome, athletic; had languishing eyes, a long mustache, and a fine figure; one was clever, almost brilliant, and what some women call "intellectual;" the third was rich, good-looking, and "successful."

None of them had any drawback; the first was clever enough; the second was very good-looking, and, like the first, was comfortably off; and the third was neither a fool nor unread. All three were considered good catches by mammas who had marriageable daughters, and were popular.

The fourth gentleman was a silent man, who kept his own counsel, went his own gait, and was thought to be independent in his fortune as he was known to be in his views.

After a season in which the young lady had been greatly and generally admired, each of the three friends, having observed the growing attachment of the other two, discovered that he was in love with her; each teased the others about her to sound them; each denied the charge, hated the others warmly for the time, and each decided to get ahead of his friends. All three made the fourth gentleman their confidant.

The society beau was the first to declare himself. He had had the best opportunities; had danced with the lady all winter; had the finest figure; had been the best-dressed man in the set; had driven a good team; and had talked easily of Browning's poems and of Kipling's stories. The occasion which presented itself to him was auspicious. It was a spring afternoon in the grounds of a beautiful country place, where an entertainment was being given by a mutual friend. The spot was secluded; the air was balmy; the flowers were dazzling; the birds sang. He was arrayed faultlessly, and he and the lady were alone. He naturally began to talk love to her, and was about to reach the point where his voice should grow deep and his look intense. He had told her of her beauty; she had listened with a pleased smile and a changing color. He felt that he almost had her. They were at the end of a long flower-bed blue with pansies, which just matched her eyes. He stooped and picked one. As he rose she said, " A race to the other end — you that side, I this," and dashed off. She ran like a doe. He had a record, and could easily have beaten her, but as they approached the other end, he saw that her path divided there. One fork ran off from him, the other turned into his. It flashed on him in a second: he would let her choose and she would run into his arms. She chose; and when they returned to the house he had her answer. He resolved to say nothing of it.

Just afterwards the second gentleman found his opportunity. It was after the intellectual entertainment. He had easily outshone all others. She had applauded him warmly, and had afterwards congratulated him. He took her into the library. Old books were about them; beautiful pictures were on the walls; the light fell tempered to the softest glow. He recognized his opportunity. He felt his intellect strong within him. He approached her skilfully: he hinted at the delights of the union of two minds perfectly attuned; he illustrated aptly by a reference to the harmony just heard and to numerous instances in literature. He talked of the charm of culture; spoke confidently of his preferment; suggested, without appearing to do so, his fortunate advantages over others, and referred, with some contempt, to commonplace men like the fourth gentleman. He praised her intellect. Her eye kindled; her form trembled; he felt his influence over her. He repeated a poem he had written her. It was good enough to have been published in a magazine. Her face glowed. He glanced up, caught her eye, and held his hand ready to receive hers. She lifted her hand, looked into his eyes, and he had his answer. They strolled back, and he determined to keep it all a secret. Passing, they happened upon the third gentleman, who spoke to her; and No. 2 a moment later left her with him.

He led the way into a little apartment just by. It seemed to have escaped the notice of the guests. It was sumptuously fitted up for a tête-à-tête. Wealth and taste had combined to make it perfect. She exclaimed with pleasure at its beauty. After handing her a chair as luxurious as art could make it, the gentleman began. He told of his home; of his enterprise; of his success; of his wealth. It had doubled year after year. It was hers. He laid before her his plans. They were large enough to be bewildering. She would be the richest woman in her acquaintance. She could be an angel with it. With mantling cheek and glowing face she bent towards him. "It is yours," he said; "all yours. You will be worth—" He paused, then stated the sum. She leaned towards him with an earnest gesture, her voice trembling as she spoke. He had his answer.

As they passed out through the corridor they met the fourth gentleman. He did not speak. He stood aside to let them pass. He glanced at her lover, but if he looked at her, she did not see it. He was evidently leaving.

"Are you going?" she said, casually, as she passed.

"Yes."

"Is it late?"

"I do not know."

She paused, and her lover politely passed on.

"Why are you going, then?"

"Because I wish to go."

"Will you take me to my chaperon?"

"With pleasure."

"With pleasure?"

"With great pleasure."

"You are not very civil."

"I had not intended to be."

"Do you think—"

"Sometimes. This evening, for instance. There is your chaperon."

"I did not think you—"

"So I supposed. You made a mistake. Good-bye."

BUYING THE WEDDING-RING

"Good-bye?"

"Yes. Good-bye."

The wedding-cards of the young lady were issued within a few weeks, and ten days later she was married. In the press accounts of the wedding the bride was spoken of as "beautiful, accomplished, clever, good, and wise." And the groom was described as "handsome, stylish, intellectual, and wealthy."

Some people said they always thought she would have married differently; some said they always knew she would marry just as she did. (These were mostly women.) She herself said that she made up her mind suddenly.

THE DANGER OF BEING TOO THOROUGH

WE had been discussing thoroughness. "Now I tell you there's such a thing as being too thorough," said the Judge. "When I first went on the bench, I determined to plumb the law every time. One of the first cases that came up before me was a suit, in one of my upper counties, for divorce, brought by a wife against her husband. The pleadings were all right, and the proof was clear—so clear, indeed, that although the defendant contested strongly, I became satisfied that there was collusion, and dismissed the suit. It created a sensation. I reached home feeling very virtuous. I was sitting on the veranda next day reading, when a man, evidently a countryman, rode up on a thin mule, and, hitching it to the fence, came in at the gate. I recognized the defendant in the divorce suit. He was dressed in his 'Sunday best,' capped by an old beaver, and was carrying a pair of saddle-bags over his arm. I invited him to take a seat, and he at once began, calling me 'your Honor.'

"'Your Honor,' he said, 'I came to see you about that divorce suit.'

"'Well, what about it?' I asked, sharply, getting ready to pitch into him; but he was so meek I held up. He just shook his head.

"'Your Honor, that was the cruelest decree your Honor ever made. You didn't know about it, or your Honor wouldn't 'a' done it. Why, your Honor, all that fuss I made was jist put on. I wanted it jist as bad as my wife. Why, we had arranged everything, and we was both ready to git married ag'in directly. We was agoin' to have a double wedding. She was agoin' to marry a sto'keeper what makes three hundred dollars a year, and I was agoin' to marry a lady as has considerable propity. She is got a hundred and twenty-three acres o' lan', and two cows, and a hoss. She broke off one engagement to marry me, and the man is a-suin' her for breach, and now she is agoin' to sue me for breach too, and I don't know what to do.' And neither did I," said the Judge: " I could hear my wife giggling inside."

" I once made a mistake myself by trying to be very thorough," said the Governor, shutting his teeth down on his Habana, and closing his eyes retrospectively.

" When was it ?" we asked.

" Not so long ago," said the Governor. " Does any of you think I look like a felon ?" he asked. The replies were not unanimous. " Well, I was arrested as one within the last two years," he said. " When I came into the governorship I thought I would be very thorough, and one of the first things I investigated was the convict-system. The newspapers said I had made promises that I would give honest labor a show. Perhaps I had. So one day I slipped off by myself and went up to the mines to see how the thing was being worked when no one was expected. The charge had been made that the lessees ran things very differently when an investigating committee was expected from the way they usually ran them, and that ordinarily the treatment was very harsh. I intended to go down into the mines, and I put on an old suit of clothes in which I used to hunt occasionally. They were torn and muddy, and I congratulated myself that no one would know me.

"In the pockets were all sorts of odds and ends, such as string, wire, a knife, nippers, etc. I got the conductor to let me off the train at a crossing, and walked a mile or two up to the mines. As I got near them, thinking I would look over the ground before going out into the cleared space, I turned out of the path and struck up the hill through the brush. I took a survey, and saw a small group of men around a fire, one or two of them convicts, one or two, perhaps, visitors, and one a guard with a double-barrelled shot-gun across his arm. I was thinking of going down, and took a step or two, when some one behind me said, 'Hold on; come back here.' I turned, and there, thirty steps from me was a guard, an ugly old fellow, long and bony, standing with his shot-gun across his arm. 'What do you want?' I asked.

"'I wants you,' he said, 'and I wants you quick. Come here.'

"I went over, moved rather by curiosity. 'Well, what do you want with me?'

" 'I'm goin' to take you to the warden,' he said.

" 'But I won't go,' I said. 'I don't want to go to the warden, and I won't go.'

" 'You won't? Well, we'll see if you won't. If you don't, you'll git a load o' buckshot in you,' he said, dropping his gun, and pulling back the hammer slowly.

"I saw that he had me, and I determined to explain. 'I am a visitor up here,' I said.

" 'Yes, no doubt; that's why I wants you. I wants you to finish out your visit. We can't bar to part with you. Walk along thar.'

" 'But—' I began.

" 'But nothing,' said he; 'you don't want no "but" but this,' and he gave me a crack with the butt of his gun which nearly knocked me over. 'March on.'

" 'Look here; I'm the Governor of the State,' said I, trying to look imposing.

"He looked at me quizzically. 'You're a pretty-looking Gov'nor, ain't you?' said he. 'Well, Gov'nor, I'm glad to see you; I'm gwine to help you finish out yo' term. Walk along thar and shet up yer jaw. I'm gittin' kinder tired on it, and I've a good mind to let

"SOME ONE BEHIND ME SAID 'HOLD ON!'"

you have a load of buckshot anyways, jest to teach you manners.'

"Well, that old fellow marched me down, and made a convict go through my clothes. The things in my pockets were proof positive of my guilt, of course, and you never heard such a lambasting as he gave me in your life, all the time keeping a running fire at me, asking what I was 'in for,' etc. The circumstantial evidence was that I was a burglar, but they all agreed I looked like a pickpocket, and one man even suggested that I had picked a burglar's pocket. That was the worst of all. Then he marched me off to the warden."

"What became of the guard?" asked one.

"He's my manager on my farm," said the Governor, "and he still makes me march straight."

UNCLE JACK'S VIEWS OF GEOGRAPHY

WHEN the war ended and the negroes were free there was a great enthusiasm for educating them. One of the first schools started was built on the edge of his place by Colonel Trigg, who got a little "school-marm," as they were termed, to come down and teach it. It was soon filled by the colored population, the pupils ranging from five to seventy-five years, all studying "a-b ab, e-b eb." Even "Uncle Jack Scott," the colonel's head man, one of the "old-timers," went in, and was transferred from the stable to the school-room. The colonel fumed about it; but it was laid to the door of Uncle Jack's new wife, "Mrs. Scott," who was a "citified" lady, and had many airs. Uncle Jack was an acquisition to the school, and was given a prominent position by the stove, the little school-mistress paying him especial attention, putting him through his "a-b ab's and e-b eb's" with much pride, and holding him up to her younger scholars as a shining example. A few days later Uncle Jack appeared, armed with a long hickory switch, which he presented to the teacher with a remark about "lazy niggers needin' hick'ry 's much 's bread," and loud enough to be heard by the whole school. Miss Barr (called "Bear" by Mrs. Scott) took the hickory with visible emotion, made a speech to the school upon Uncle Jack's wisdom and appreciation of educational advantages, and Uncle Jack, with much grandeur, went to his task. The lesson that day was "b-a ba, b-e be." Unhappily, Uncle Jack had learned "a-b ab, e-b eb" too well, and b and a were never anything but ab, and b and e never anything but eb, no matter in what order they came. Miss Barr was at her wits' end. She had established her rules, and she stood by them. Had she believed it her duty, she would have gone to perdition without a tremor. One of her most invariable rules was to thrash for missing lessons. When Uncle Jack missed his lesson two days hand-running, she was in despair; but discipline was to be preserved, and after hours of painful suspense, when he still failed, she ordered him to stand up. He obeyed. She glanced around, seeking some alternative; fifty pairs of eyes were fastened upon her. She reached under her desk, and slowly drew out a hickory, the very one Uncle Jack had brought her. Fifty pairs of eyes showed their whites.

"Take off your coat."

There was a gasp throughout the room.

Uncle Jack paused a moment as if stupefied, then laid down his book and took off his coat.

"Take off your waistcoat."

He obeyed.

"You ain't gwine meck me teck off my shirt, is you?" he asked, tremulously.

"No. Clasp your hands."

He did so, and she raised the hickory and brought it down "swauo" across his back. Again there was a gasp throughout the room, which came every time a lick was given. Uncle Jack was the only one who uttered no sound. He stood like a statue. When she finished, he put on his coat and sat down. School was dismissed.

"'TAKE OFF YOUR COAT'"

Next day Uncle Jack was at his old place at the stable.

"Why, I thought you were at school?" said his master, who had heard something of the trouble.

"Nor, suh; I got 'nough edication," he said. He stuck his curry-comb into his brush. There was a pause; then: "I tell you de fac', Marse Conn. I is too ole to be whupt by a ooman, an' a po' white ooman at dat."

It was several years after this that Uncle Jack was working one day at a water-gate in a field, when the children came down the road from school. They stopped and peeped stolidly through the fence. Among them was "Jawnie," Mrs. Scott's hopeful, who had proved an apter scholar than his father. His bag was on his arm. He climbed over the fence, and from the bank gazed down apathetically at his father in the water below. Presently he said:

"Or, poppa, de teacher say you mus' git me a geography."

Uncle Jack's jaw set. He dug on as if he had not heard. Then he repeated to himself: "Geog'aphy—geog'aphy. Marse Conn, whut is dat? Whut is a geog'aphy?" he asked, looking up at his employer, who happened to be by.

"A geography?" said the Colonel. "Why, a geography is a—is a book—a book that tells about places, and where they are, and so on." He gave a comprehensive sweep with his arm around the horizon.

"Yas, suh; now I onderstands," said Jack, going back to digging.

Presently he stopped, and looked up at "Jawnie." "I say, boy, you tell de teacher *I* say you better stick to you' a-b ab's an' you' e-b eb's, an' let geog'aphy alone. You knows de way now to de spring an' de wood-pile an' de mill, an' when you gits a little bigger I's gwine to show you de way to de hoe-handle an' de cawn-furrer, an' dat's all de geog'aphy a nigger's got to know."

He dug on.

BILLINGTON'S VALENTINE

It was St. Valentine's day, and, owing to an engagement to go duck-shooting, Billington had taken a holiday. The storm had, however, broken up the shooting, and Billington was now seated in the sitting-room of his apartments, alone except for his own thoughts. The rain outside spattering in fitful showers against the windows, and the fact that all his bets had gone wrong for several days past, had inclined him to be serious, and two valentines he had just received completed the work.

For an hour he had been engaged in that dismal occupation of looking himself squarely in the face.

Both presents were cigar-cases, and the messages on the two cards were identical—simply these words: " From St. Valentine." One of the cases was solid silver, exquisitely chased, and engraved with Billington's crest and coat of arms; the other was simply two bits of flexible card-board covered and bound together with a piece of old brocade, on which was embroidered a sprig of apple blossoms.

"I wish I had the courage," said Billington, for the twentieth time. He half turned and looked at the two cases, and presently stretched out his arm lazily to take up one of them. At first, his hand hovered over the embroidered one, but the beautiful chasing on the other struck him, and he leaned over and took up that. "Very handsome," he said to himself, inspecting it. "That girl has a great deal of taste. So that was the reason she wanted to see my coat of arms." He reached over and put the case down carefully, and after a second's reflection picked up the other. "That's a really lovely thing," he said; "those apple blossoms are perfect. She made that herself, and—by Jove, that's a piece of the old dress she wore that night at the Valentine ball ten years ago!" He leaned his head back and shut his eyes. "Lord! Lord! How sweet she was that night!" he said, with his eyes still shut. "She seventeen, and I twenty-five. I remember I told her she had the spirit of her great-grandmother in her, and she said, No, she had only her dress on her. I remember I did not have the money to buy her flowers, and I went and found her a bunch of apple blossoms that had come out in the warm spell. I told her it was a miracle performed for her; and they were the only flowers she wore. I did not ask her to marry me, because I did not feel that I had a right to do it till I could support her; and then I came off to New York to—get able." Here he stopped, and his countenance changed.

"Well, I got her the place at the Institute," he said, in a defensive tone. Once more he leaned his head back. "Let me see; what was the old rhyme I repeated to her that night?

> 'Roses are red, violets are blue,
> Pinks are sweet, and so are you.'

And that other?

> 'Tumdy, tumdy, tumdy tine.'

Ah! this is it:

> 'As sure as the bloom grows on the vine,
> I'll choose you for my Valentine.'"

He lapsed into silence, and after a second

got up slowly, and walked about the room with his hands deep in his pockets. Catching sight of himself in a mirror, he stopped and gazed at himself earnestly. "What a cursed ugly thing a man is!" he said, turning away. He flung himself into his chair again, and retired within himself once more. Suddenly he sat up. "By Jove, I'll do it!" he said. "In five years I won't be fit for any woman to have."

He reached over and took a sheet of paper and a pen; dipped his pen in his silver inkstand, and with a look of determination on his face squared himself to write. "St. Valentine's day," he began, and paused. A look of perplexity came on his face, which deepened into one of worry. He laid the pen down. "Which one?" he said to himself, half audibly. He looked into the fire. "Oh, hang it! I'll write a valentine," he said; and dipping the pen into the ink again, he began to write briskly:

> "My patron saint, St. Valentine,
> Why dost thou leave me to repine,
> Still supplicating at her shrine?

"'I FOUND HER A BUNCH OF APPLE BLOSSOMS'"

"But bid her eyes to me incline,
 I'll ask no other sun to shine,
 More rich than is Golconda's mine.

"Range all that woman, song, or wine
 Can give; wealth, power, and fame combine;
 For her I'd gladly all resign.

"Take all the pearls are in the brine,
 Sift heaven for stars, earth's flowers entwine,
 But be her heart my Valentine."

Here he stopped and read it over. "That's pretty good for an off-hand effort," he said to himself. He read it over again. "'More rich than is Golconda's mine,'" he repeated. "I wonder if that could be considered personal? 'For her I'd gladly all resign,'" he read. "By Jove, this would do for either." He leaned back, and the same expression his face had worn a little while before came back on it. Suddenly, with a growl, he sat up and began again; but his pen would no longer go. Only the old rhyme rang in his head:

"Roses are red, violets are blue,
 Pinks are sweet, and so are you."

He picked up the embroidered case and

looked at it. As he did so he seemed to catch
a faint odor of apple blossoms, and he actually
lifted the case to his face to see if it were only
fancy. Ah, if he had only had then a fourth
of what he had now, how different it might
have been! Now he made ten thousand a
year, but wanted fifty thousand. He put the
case down and picked up the silver one. Fifty
thousand! Horses, equipages, books, paint-
ings, travel, honors — everything almost — except the perfume of those apple blossoms. He
laid the case down and took up his pen. He
had in mind such rhymes as "line," "thine;"
"resign," "entwine;" but the old verse,

"As sure as the bloom grows on the vine,
I'll choose you for my Valentine,"

drove out all others. Once more there came
that subtile perfume of the apple blossoms.
There seemed to be a sudden lighting up. He
gazed out of the window, and became aware
that the rain had stopped and the sun was
shining.

"Oh, hang it!" he said, "I'll go to walk."
He folded up his valentine, and, putting it into
an envelope, he placed it in his pocket unad-

dressed. He went out, and strolled up the Avenue, looking at the pretty girls whom the sunshine had brought out like so many flowers. Presently, he stepped into a florist's and bought a large bunch of glorious roses, great rich, crimson buds with long stems, each fit for a princess to wear. He paid for them, and gave the address to which he wished them sent. The price, he thought, half grimly, was more than his month's board used to cost. This almost interfered with the other thought that twenty-five dollars was a small matter with him now. He took out the valentine, and picked up a pen to address it; but put it back into his pocket again unaddressed, and continued his stroll, bowing to men, and bowing and smiling to girls he met. He went on into the Park. There was a faint hint of green in some favored spots, and, to his surprise, as he passed on, he came on a little bush in blossom — an apple bush. It grew in a sunny nook sheltered from the north, and by one of those freaks of nature, in the warm humid days that had come it had been dreaming of the spring, and one bough had blown into full bloom. Billington stopped with a sudden thrill of pleased surprise, and, climbing down the bank, he broke off the apple bough —his pleasure rather heightened by the reflection that a policeman might arrest him: it reminded him of his boyhood.

As he strolled back down the Avenue the sidewalks were gay with walkers, and showy equipages with fine horses and pompous coachmen rolled by with all the livery of wealth. Billington was just admiring a handsome pair of strange sorrels to a new brougham, when he became aware that the coachman was drawing up to him. He looked at the carriage, and in it sat one of the subjects of his thoughts that morning. She had never looked handsomer, and when she gave him her daintily gloved hand with a cordial pressure, Billington had never liked her better.

"I never saw such an abstracted air," she laughed. "I really thought you were not going to speak to me."

"I was thinking of you at the time—I believe," said Billington, wondering if only a part of the truth were not a lie. He condoned with his conscience by adding a whole truth. "I was just wondering whose turnout this was, and thinking it the handsomest on the Avenue."

"Isn't it lovely!" she said. "Papa gave it to me as a valentine. Aren't those sorrels darlings?" Billington could truthfully say that they were. He was reminded of the card-case, and he thanked her very warmly, and was pleased to see the color deepen in her face. She did not often color.

"You will find a valentine for you at home when you get back, I suspect," he said.

"What is it?" she asked, eagerly.

"The only thing in town worthy of your acceptance after those horses," said Billington.

"I don't know about that," she said, with more coyness in her manner than she often showed. Billington wished he had sent the verses along with the roses.

"Don't you want to take a little drive in the Park?" she asked, moving her seal-skin robe a little. Billington was just going to say that nothing would give him more pleasure, when, glancing up, he saw one whom he had not seen for quite a little while, but who had been in his thoughts oftener than once that morning. She was not strolling at the holiday pace of the richly dressed throng of pleasure-seekers, but was tripping along at a most business-like gait, threading her way in and out among the saunterers. As she passed Billington she glanced up and saw him, and a smile of recognition lit up her face.

"Good-morning," she smiled, and tripped on.

"What a very pretty woman!" said the girl in the carriage. "And such a pretty frock and hat too! Who is she?"

"She is a young artist," said Billington, still following with his eye the neat, trim figure working its way along through the throng on the sidewalk. "I have known her a long time." "For her I'd gladly all resign," sprang a verse into his mind.

"Can she paint?" asked the girl.

"Ah—really, I don't believe I know," said Billington. "I know she has ability."

"Well, come on, get in," she said, moving, and making room for him beside her.

"Ah—no, I believe I can't go," said Billington. "I'd like to do so some other time, but I have been to the Park, and I have to go down and attend to a matter. Good-bye."

"Good-bye; I hope to see you soon. What are you going to do this evening? Why not come home to dinner with us?"

The impatient horses started off too quickly for Billington to speak his reply, so he simply smiled and bowed it after her.

He looked down the Avenue, but could not see the person he was looking for; when the carriage drew off his attention, he had lost her. He was just about to curse his luck, when he caught sight of her again crossing the street. The next minute Billington was spinning down the street. The light that came into her face and the pleased tone in her voice when he overtook her made a warm glow come about his heart.

"I thought I had lost you," he said, almost out of breath.

"I did not think you wished not to," she answered, with a look half mischief, half inquiry. "Wasn't that Miss Van Sheckeldt?"

"Yes;" and to prevent further investigation he said, "Won't you let me give you these?" He handed her the apple blossoms.

"Oh, how lovely!" she exclaimed as she took them. "Apple blossoms, upon my word!

Where on earth did you get them?" She was holding them off and turning them around at arm's-length to admire them. " I wanted just these very things to finish a painting I am on of 'Spring Captive.' Do you know, I believe you can perform miracles?"

"I don't see that you needed them," said Billington. " You can create them. Do you know that your needle has the soul of an artist in it?"

"I don't know; I am glad you think so, though. I was afraid I had not got them exactly right, and I wanted them to be just right. I wanted to show my appreciation of all your kindness to me since we have known each other."

Billington felt a good deal more than he said, and more than he hoped he showed.

She broke off a sprig of the blossoms and placed it in her bosom. The act and the unconscious grace with which she did it carried him back ten years. The perfume of the blossoms stole in upon his senses.

"Won't you go to walk with me?" he asked her, earnestly.

" Oh, I'd like to do it, but I cannot. I have

my class. You know I am a teacher now," she said, proudly. "The place you got me has done everything for me, and the prize I got enabled me to get the place I have. Well, here's my place. By-the-way, Miss Van Sheckeldt's father is the new trustee. Good-bye."

She had shaken hands with him and was gone up the steps before Billington was aware that it was beginning to shower. Billington strolled across to the flower-shop to get out of the rain, but just as he reached the door some one called him. He turned as Miss Van Sheckeldt's carriage rolled up.

"Let me take you home," she said. "I caught you! Whom were you going to order flowers for?" she asked, laughing.

"For no one; they are ordered," he said; "and remember, they were ordered before I saw you this morning."

"Come and confide in me, and save the gloss on that immaculate hat," she said; and Billington sprang in, pulled up the seal-skin robe, and drove off by her side as the rain began to pour.

That afternoon he addressed his valentine.

His friends all declare it was a true love match.

SHE HAD ON HER GERANIUM LEAVES

WHEN Buck left college it was with the reputation of being the wildest, cleverest, and most worthless man in our class, that is, reckless.

"There is no security in the world like the reputation of being worthless," he used to say. "With it a man can talk love to any girl he pleases, and the girl likes him, too."

The next thing I heard of him he was practising law at the county-seat of his native county, and it was said that he had one side or the other of every case, and was madly in love with the pretty daughter of the rector of the parish. The next thing I heard was a rumor that he had "held up some man" on the street one night and had been forced to run away from the State. I did not believe the robbery story; but there was a mystery about it.

It was several years after this that I happened to be in a new town in the Southwest. I registered at the Plaza, the new plank hotel, and had eaten my supper and was about to retire, when there was a heavy tread outside of my room. The door opened without the ceremony of a knock, and a tall, fine-looking man, with a black slouched hat, full camp rig, and a cigar in his mouth, walked in. It was Buck. I knew him in a second by his smile. He had not changed a whit. He was the chief engineer of the new railroad. I asked him how he came to leave his old home.

His eyes twinkled. "Got religion, and could not stand the law."

"I heard you could not stand the law," I said; "but I did not hear it was religion. I heard it was holding a man up—robbery."

"It was," he said—"of his girl. You know I used to be a deuce of a fool about women; am one now, for that matter, about one, at least; would not give a cent for a man who was not. Well, I used to be awfully in love with a little girl—the preacher's daughter.

Pretty as a puppy! She liked me, too; but I used to kind of knock liquor those days, and her old folks were down on me. That was all right; and at last she began to try to save me. I had her then. Nothing to help a man with a woman like having her try to save him. Well, I was getting along all right; but she had a fellow coming to see her, an old fellow from town with a big pile. I had seen him once or twice before, and I took it into my head that she was liking him. I got to cutting up about it, and the first thing I knew she had sent me flying. I got on a spree, and stayed there till I heard one evening that he had come to see her. I sobered up, and went around to the hotel to find out about him. I found that he had taken the private parlor, and had sent a note around by Link to my girl. Link was my nigger. I owned him body and soul; he would have committed murder for me. So I got hold of him and cross-questioned him. The snow was on the ground, and I found Frasher had written to ask Miss Lizzie to go sleigh-riding with him.

"'Did she look pleased?' I asked Link.

"'Yas, suh, dat she did ; an' I hear' her calling Mincie to meck up good fire in de parlor toreckly.'

"I swore. I think I did. I believe I used to swear in those days."

"I believe you did. Go on," I said.

"Well, Link noticed it and consoled me.

"'He gwine teck her sleigh-ridin' by moonlight. He up-stairs gitting ready now.'

"I gave Link a quarter and went to supper. Link went up to answer the old fellow's call, and to tell him a lot of lies about me. When he came down to supper Ben Brice told him a lot more. For one thing, he told him that I had gone crazy from love of Miss Lizzie, and had tried to commit two wanton murders out of pure jealousy, and had been acquitted on the ground of insanity. I went to the doctor's whilst he was at supper and asked for Miss Lizzie. She sent down word that she had a headache and requested to be excused. I sent her word back that I wanted to take her sleigh-riding. She replied that she could not go. Both lamps were lighted in the parlor, and the fire was blazing. I went back up to the hotel and borrowed Ben Brice's old horse-pistol, got a bottle of whiskey, and went down to the doctor's again to mount guard at the gate. I had just reached the gate when the sleigh drove up with the old fellow in it under a big buffalo robe, and Link by his side to hold the horses. He stepped out and started to go into the gate.

"'Halt!' says I.

"He did so, and asked what I wanted. I told him that he could not go in there, that Miss Lizzie was sick.

"'Why, I have an engagement to go sleigh-riding with her,' he said.

"I told him that I knew that; but I had later intelligence, and she was too unwell to go out that evening. I had it from her own lips, and as her friend I could not allow her to be disturbed. This set him back a good deal; but he began to bluster. He 'would go in there,' and he 'wished to know who I was,' etc. I just pulled out my old pistol and shoved it up under his nose. You ought to have seen him! A keg of powder could not have set it off, but it looked like a cannon. Then I began to lecture him on the sin of persecuting a poor girl like he was doing—an old thing

"HE WAS AS MELLOW AS AN APPLE"

with a dyed mustache like him. You never heard such a lecture in your life. I preached like the doctor. Presently he said he would go back to the hotel, he was catching cold. I told him no, I could not let him go back just yet, but that I had some whiskey. He said he never touched whiskey. I told him that neither did I, but I had brought this along to keep him from catching cold, and he must drink it. He turned to Link and asked him in an undertone if he thought I really would shoot him.

"'Yas, suh,' said Link. 'Marse Buck 'ain't got a bit better sense 'n to shoot you. He 'ain't got no sense about shooting folks, noway.'

"Well, sir, you never saw such a drink as he took. I don't believe he had had a drop in a year. I thought he was going to the bottom of the bottle. The next thing I did, I chucked him into the sleigh, and jumped in after him. Link jumped out as I grabbed the reins, and the horses went off with a bolt. They were the finest sleigh team you ever saw, and I let 'em go. You never heard a man pray so in all your life. When we got back it was about half-past eleven, and he was as mellow as an apple. I put him to bed, and went down to the doctor's. The lights were still burning in the parlor, and I walked in. Miss Lizzie was sitting before the fire with her little red shoes on the fender and her furs on a chair, pretending to read. I told her she had just as well take off those geranium leaves and put out those lights; that her old beau with his dyed mustache was in bed drunk, and his team had had all the moonlight driving they could stand that night. Whoop! but she was mad. She never spoke to me till I went back there; but she never spoke to him again at all. He went home next day, and died soon afterwards. Ben Brice said it was pneumonia; but I don't think it was. Lizzie and I both agree it was old age."

Just then the door opened, and a black negro with a jolly face poked his head in, and said, with his teeth shining, "Marse Buck, Miss Lizzie say you can bring de gent'man up now; she done put on her geramium leabes."

A STORY OF CHARLES HARRIS

There are few of us who ever knew Charlie Harris who will not remember him best as "Chad," the faithful, fat, and delightful body-servant, friend, and guardian of Colonel Carter of Cartersville. His soft dialect, his mushy accent, his natural gestures, his limp, long since forgotten, but put on again when his master recalled the heroic incident in which he received the bullet in his leg, all combined to make him the only real "nigger" on the stage. But to know Charlie Harris truly one had to know him off the stage.

One night at the rooms of some friends high up on Fifth Avenue we got him to talking about old times and his life in Louisiana. "Boys, if you think I am a good 'nigger,' you ought to see me as a villain. You do not know what a villanous villain I am. It was the first character I ever played," he said. Then he told us. He had not been playing long when his company went to New Orleans. His old home was near there, and one day his old mammy and her husband, "Uncle Tony," called on him. They had come down from the country to see him. He invited them to come and see him play that night, and sent them front seats in the colored people's gallery. "They thought I owned the theatre," he said, "and expected to see me looking like a king at the Mardigras. Well, in the piece that night I was the villain. I was not made up much, and consequently I could be easily recognized. I cut my eye up towards the gallery as I entered, and saw the old folks in their places. Uncle Tony knew me at once, for he undertook to point me out to mammy. I could hear him describing me. 'Dat's him. Nor, not dat one; *dat* one—dat fat one over dyah.' Presently mammy saw me and made a gesture to me. Well, I was the meanest rascal in that play you ever saw—as cold as a lizard and as calculating as a rat. I cheated every one, and everybody hated me. For a time I succeeded, but after a period of prosperity I was at last found out, and everybody jumped on me. I was caught stealing, and was abused like a pickpocket

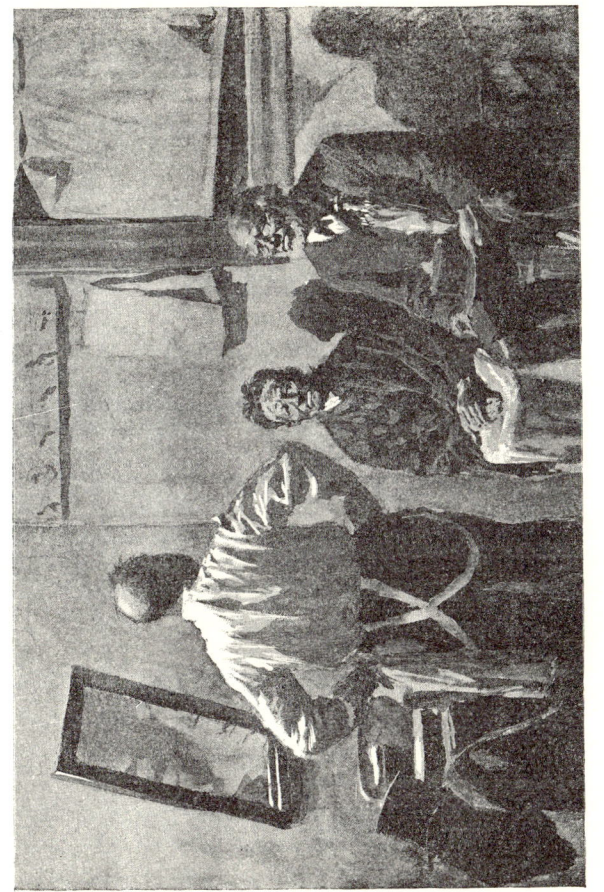

"YOUR PA NEVER WOULD STOOD NO SICH 'THING AS DAT'"

without a word to say for myself. In the middle of it I heard an exclamation from the gallery, and caught a glimpse of Uncle Tony and mammy. They were both leaning far over the rail in great excitement. Just then I was seized and banged around the room by the hero. I was too busy to notice more than that both mammy and Uncle Tony were on their feet gesticulating; but just as I was being hustled to the door to be kicked out, I heard a scream, 'Yo'-all let my chile alone!' and a deeper voice shouting, 'Knock him down, Marse Charlie, knock him down! Wait; I'm comin'.' Then the door closed on me, and a storm of applause went through the house.

"When the play was over, some one told me that two old negroes were waiting outside to see me. I had them shown in. I saw that something was the matter, and tried to be jocular, but it was too serious with them. Mammy was whimpering and, with arms folded tightly, was rocking from side to side, and Uncle Tony was as solemn as a tombstone. 'Marse Charlie, you didn't steal dem things sho 'nough, did you?' asked Uncle

Tony, whilst mammy rocked and moaned. 'No,' I exclaimed, 'of course not.' 'I tole you so; I tole you so,' said mammy. 'I tole dem other niggers so up dem stairs dyah. 'Twas dat other man heself—I tole em so.' I tried to explain, for I saw my danger. I had played too naturally. It never had occurred to me that they would think me a thief. I was not entirely successful, however. 'Marse Charlie, your pa never would 'a' stood no sich thing as dat,' said Uncle Tony. ' He never 'd 'a' let no man lay a han' 'pon him in dis wull!' 'Why, that was in the play,' I explained. 'Don't you see?' 'Mighty curiousome sort of play,' said Uncle Tony, solemnly. 'Have a man knock you down and stomp all over you like dat, and then dar'sn' even raise your han' 'bout it. I bound your pa would 'a' knocked his head offn any man that laid his han' 'pon him.' 'Well, he 'bleeged to git a livin',' said mammy, apologetically. 'Mighty hard way to git a livin',' said Uncle Tony, suspiciously. ' I glad old marster 'ain' know nuttin' 'bout it, dat's all.' They went out. They are both dead now,' said Charlie, softly.

And now Charlie is dead too.

HE WOULD HAVE GOTTEN A LAWYER

I was attending the term of Henrico court one spring when I had been at the bar only a year or two, and was in the court-room when the criminal docket was called. The clerk read out the case of "The Commonwealth *vs.* Mannie Johnson: an indictment for a felony," and my attention was arrested by hearing the sheriff say the prisoner had no counsel. If there is one thing which excites the sympathy of a young lawyer, it is a prisoner who has no counsel. There was a little colloquy between the judge, the commonwealth's attorney, and the sheriff, and the judge finally said, "Well, bring him in, anyhow; I will see about it."

The long-legged, gangling sheriff retired, and in a little while re-entered with his most professional solemnity about him, preceded by a stumpy, little, rusty, bow-legged negro, about thirty-five years of age and about five feet in height, who looked, perhaps, as unlikely to be able to steal a steer as anybody in the world.

The sheriff roughly pointed out a chair to him, and he sat down in it without even taking a look at the jury lounging in their box.

" Is that the man ?" asked the judge. " Did that man steal a steer ?"

The sheriff smiled the smile of one familiar with the classes who steal steers; the commonwealth's attorney smiled with the smile of one who makes ten dollars out of each indictment for a felony which he is able to draw and get a grand jury to find; even the jury smiled; I know I smiled. The prisoner, with his old ragged hat in his hand, was the only one who did not smile. He glanced up for a second at the judge on the bench, then dropped his eyes to a level, and sat as motionless as before.

" Have you any counsel ?" asked the judge. The prisoner looked at him, but said nothing; and the judge, appreciating the fact that he perhaps did not understand the question, asked him, " Have you any lawyer ?"

" Nor, suh," he said, twisting a little in his seat, and settling down as before.

The judge turned to me and asked me to defend him, adding, civilly, "if my other clients could wait a little while." I informed him that I thought my other clients could wait; that I always made my clients wait my own pleasure (they had then been waiting some months); and going around, took a seat approximately near to my new client's side.

"Have you any witnesses?" I asked.

He did not look at me, or, if he did, it was only a glance; he simply said, "Nor, suh."

"Can you get any if I get a continuance— if I get the case put off till next month?"

"I don' know;—nor, suh," he said, scarcely taking the trouble to speak.

"Well," I said, rising, "I think we are ready; we might as well go into trial."

The jury was waked up and sworn. The clerk made the prisoner stand up, and read an indictment as long as himself, and the commonwealth's attorney called his witnesses. There were five of them.

The first was a farmer, who testified that he owned the steer in question, and that one evening he saw him in his pasture when he attended to his stock, and the following morning when he went out he missed him. He thought at first that he might have fallen into a ditch, but not finding him, he went around the fence, and finally found his tracks going out of the gate and down the road towards Richmond, followed by the tracks of a man who was evidently driving him. He got his horse and followed in hot haste, but the steer had evidently been stolen early in the night, and he did not overtake him until he got to town; there, after some hunting, he found him in the possession of a butcher, who claimed to have bought him from the negro now at the bar.

The butcher himself was sworn, and testified that early one morning the prisoner drove the steer up to his gate, claiming it to be his, and stating that he wanted some money very badly, in consideration of which he, the butcher, gave him fifteen dollars for the steer.

The other witnesses were two men who happened to be present, and who identified the prisoner as the person who sold the butcher the steer, and the policeman who made the arrest, and who testified to something which the commonwealth's attorney called "a confession."

"'EF I HAD, I'D 'A' GOT ME A LAWYER'"

I asked for several instructions, which the judge, very unjustly, as I thought at that time, refused positively to give. I am bound to say now that my views upon this matter have become modified by time. I cross-examined the witnesses with much severity. Then the commonwealth's attorney made a few remarks, stating that it was not necessary to make a speech, as the evidence was all one way. And then I entered upon my argument.

I made what I deemed a very able and eloquent defence. I charged all five witnesses with perjury, and proved it to my complete satisfaction. The jury, I am bound to say, were flattering in their attention. Only a few of them dozed. When I closed, the commonwealth's attorney rose, and commented upon my argument in a way which came very near bringing on a personal collision in court between him and myself.

Then the jury retired, and returned so promptly that I felt a glow of enthusiasm that they should have hesitated so short a time, even after my able defence. The clerk took the indictment and read the verdict:

"We, the jury, find the prisoner guilty, and

sentence him to the penitentiary for ten years."

I was scarcely able to believe my own senses. I arose immediately, and, with some heat, moved to set the verdict aside on the ground that it was contrary to the evidence. This the judge refused to do, and I excepted. My client never blinked; he simply sat immobile as ever; but I was outraged. I turned to him and said,

" Well, I did the best I could for you."

He grunted, but did not look at me, and I felt that he was overcome with emotion at what I had done for him, and said:

"The only thing for us to do now is to get an appeal. I will take it up to the higher court, and fight it through for you. But it will take some money, because there are costs, and of course you ought to pay me a fee if you can. Have you got any money at all?"

Without looking at me, he said, "Nor, sur; ef I had, I'd 'a' got me a lawyer!"

I have become satisfied that he ought to have gone to the penitentiary, but the sheriff informed me afterwards that he got out of jail that night.

HOW ANDREW CARRIED THE PRECINCT

A POLITICAL STORY WITHOUT POLITICS

Andrew and Pettigrew were about equally well known in the county. They had both belonged to the same estate as boys, but their lives had been as different as their persons. Pettigrew was a slender, small, keen-looking, bright mulatto, who had been house-servant and had picked up a good deal of information, including both reading and writing, of which he was as vain as he was of his slim figure and bushy hair. Andrew was a big, black, raw-boned creature, as dull as he was ugly, and as ungainly as he was tall. He had been cow-boy till he grew too big, and then he became a steer-driver. It was to this position, coupled with his easy good-nature, that was due the intimacy between him and his young master, out of which possibly grew the following incident.

His "marse Johnnie" had always declared that Andrew had "more sense than people gave him credit for," which did not necessarily imply great wisdom. Between Andrew and Pettigrew there had always existed a strong enmity, and the small mulatto frequently exercised his ingenuity to tease and worry "that ugly, black, big-moufed nigger." Only once did he carry it too far. Andrew got him to write a valentine for him to his sweetheart, a young house-girl in the family, and when Andrew delivered it, it turned out to be a ridiculous piece of nonsense, which brought down upon her black lover her lasting anger. Pettigrew thought it a good joke, and boasted of it, but Andrew suddenly struck out. He would perhaps in his fury have broken Pettigrew's neck, had not his young master come up at the moment and saved him. Pettigrew never forgot it.

After the war Pettigrew turned out to be a great politician, and, with his accomplishments, became quite a leader in his county. Andrew was one of the very few negroes who stood by their masters. He declared that he was "a gent'man," and was going "to vote wid de gent'mens," and he did. It subjected him to no little obloquy and trouble, and his temper and health both suffered.

The county was a very close one, and for several reasons was an important one in the district, and Pettigrew, as "boss" in it, became a man of prominence. His precinct was talked of even in other counties. Only Andrew, of all his color who voted there, withstood him. The latter possessed a certain influence due to a singular circumstance. He claimed to see spirits, and to have the gift of prophecy. His habit of roaming about at night, his fearlessness of graveyards, and a certain unusual knowledge of the weather, coupled with his singular appearance and his moody look, gave him credence, and he was not a little feared in the county. This saved him from trouble which he would otherwise have had, and he remained only ostracized by those who, had they not been afraid of him, would have taken more active steps.

Finally Pettigrew, as a reward for his services, was given a position as warden in a negro insane asylum. He had not been there long when it began to be rumored in the old county that Andrew was going crazy. Pettigrew himself, who happened to be at home, was present at the examination, and testified to a number of facts which went far to establish the charge of insanity. Wandering about at night, familiarity with spirits, a claim to the gift of prophecy, all were proved. Andrew, when asked if he wished to say anything, said he was a trapper—that a graveyard was a good place for 'possums and old hares; that he sometimes saw spirits, it was true, but he never troubled them and they never bothered him; and that Pettigrew was a liar. The negro magistrates, with "Brother Johnson" at their head, decided that Andrew was crazy, and sent him on.

There was an election coming on, and Pettigrew himself could not take Andrew to the asylum; but he told him he would be there soon, and he would attend to him; and he kept his word. Andrew was reported so often for refractoriness under Pettigrew's wardenship, and appeared to be getting constantly so much worse, that finally he was removed to another ward, and, to the surprise of every one, was soon pronounced convalescent. In due time, indeed, he was declared well enough to go home for a while, and was released on trial. The report soon came back that he was entirely well.

Some months after this, however, the next election came on. It was deemed very close, and every precinct in the State counted. Andrew's "young Marse Johnnie" was a candidate in his county, and it was known that Andrew was working for him and was having much effect, notwithstanding the threats against him. Pettigrew was put up to run against him.

Pettigrew, some little time before the election, went home. In a little while came the announcement that it might be better to send and bring Andrew back to the asylum. Pettigrew said he would take him. Two nights before the election a large meeting was held in a colored church not far from the voting-place, and it was rumored that Andrew was not crazy at all, and that Pettigrew had persuaded him "to vote right." Pettigrew appeared, and made a telling speech, announcing Andrew's conversion, and that he would appear the following evening and make a full recantation of his errors "befo' de meetin'."

The following evening, just at dusk, the hour appointed, Pettigrew repaired to the rendezvous, at the junction of two paths, and awaited his convert. He had in his hand a book and writing materials to make out a list of the voters. He was just becoming impatient when he heard his man coming down the path through the pines. "I jest gwine to give you up," he said, threateningly.

"Well, heah me," said Andrew.

"Yaas, heah you!" said Pettigrew, severely. "Ef you hadn't been heah, you know what I'd done wid you?"

"Yaas, I know," said Andrew.

"You done 'member the times I done laid hick'ry upon yo' back, down yonder, 'ain't you?"

"Yaas, I 'member," said Andrew, meekly.

"Well, now, come 'long, an' don' you open yo' mouf 'cep' as I tells you ; if you does, I'll—"
He made an expressive gesture, as if he held a whip in his hand, and turned down the path through the pines, Andrew walking meekly behind him. They were in a little bottom, Pettigrew still walking before, when a noosed rope was suddenly thrown over his head from behind and jerked tight, and he was slung

down on his back, with Andrew's little black eyes close to his face.

"Ef you say a word, I'll kill you right heah," he said, and his big hands on Pettigrew's throat proved his intention. In a minute more the mulatto's arms were tightly pinioned, and then the lunatic lifted him to his feet and said, "Walk!"

The mulatto came near fainting with fear, but he walked till he got to a small stream, his first fright somewhat relieved, as they were going out towards the road.

"Wade!" said Andrew; and he waded in. Half-way across, Andrew turned him at right angles and made him wade down-stream, bowing low under the bushes which lined its banks. Deeper and deeper into the pines they penetrated, Pettigrew growing more and more alarmed; but the faintest hesitation to obey his captor's command brought the big hands to his throat with a dangerous clutch. Half a mile down the stream Andrew ordered him to turn up a smaller branch, and a hundred or two yards up he lifted him to his shoulder as easily as he would have done a child, and walking out, pushed upward into the pines. Presently they came to a heavier thicket, and stooping low and making his way through the thorn bushes, Andrew set him down in a little cleared spot. Pettigrew's eyes nearly popped from their sockets; for by the dim light of the stars he saw the dull white of a number of old tombstones, and recognized the fact that he was in an old graveyard which was known throughout the country as being the worst spot for "harnts" in that section.

Andrew set him against a small tree, around which he wrapped the end of the rope that bound him, and then took his seat on a fallen log just before Pettigrew, and looked at him silently. Presently he said, quietly, "You kin talk now." But he was mistaken; the mulatto's mouth was dry and his tongue parched.

"Why'n't you talk?" asked Andrew, calmly.

Pettigrew's teeth chattered.

"You cold?" said Andrew. "I'll warm you." He arose and began to gather sticks. Pettigrew thought he might slip away, and glanced around. His captor appeared to divine his intention, for he suddenly came back to him, and, rearranging the rope differently, made fast the end of it to the tree behind him.

"'YOU COLD? I'LL WARM YOU'"

"Don't you try it," he said, threateningly.

The divination of his thought struck the mulatto with more terror than all that had gone before. When the fire was kindled Andrew drew up his log and sat down again opposite his captive. Presently he said:

"Le' me heah what you warn me to tell de meetin'."

"I don' warn you to tell 'em nuttin," said Pettigrew.

"Yaas, you does," said Andrew; "'cause you said so. Didn't you say so?"

"Yaas, but I don' warn it now." A gleam struck him. "Andrew," he said, "ef you'll le' me off I won't trouble you no more; I won't take you back to the 'sylum. I'll let you 'lone; I swah I will."

Andrew looked at him in contempt. "Humph!" he grunted. "Le' me heah you speak."

Pettigrew remained silent.

"Say yo' pra'rs, den," muttered Andrew. He leaned over, picked up a burning chunk from the fire, and walked around towards his prisoner.

Pettigrew's eyes popped. "I'll speak," he said.

"All right; begin." Andrew sat down again and stuck the chunk back into the embers.

Pettigrew began, stammeringly enough, and said his prepared speech, "Muh fellow-citizens" and all. He made no mention of Andrew.

"Tell 'em 'bout me," said Andrew.

"What mus' I tell 'em?"

"Tell 'em what a nice white gent'man I is."

His captive uttered a few sentences sufficiently laudatory.

"Dat's enuff," said Andrew, presently. "Now tell 'em how you gwine treat me down yonder at de 'sylum."

Pettigrew protested, but the chunk of fire came out again.

"How many licks you hit me down dar?" asked Andrew.

"I—I—I don' know; I mighty sorry I hit you any."

"I is too," said Andrew. "I don' know how many dey wuz, but I know 'twuz mo'n a hunderd; I know dat; an' I gwine hit you a clean hunderd to even 'em up."

He arose, and turning, cut a bunch of stout

switches. Suddenly a thought seemed to strike him. "You see dem switches?" he said, pointing at them where they lay on the ground. "Well, I warn you to write me a letter, an' ef you'll write it right, mebby I'll let you off; *mebby* I will. You know you writes mighty good, 'cause you's got a heap o' eddication. You wuz brought up in de house, an' I warn't nuttin but a steer-driver. You's a yaller man, an' I ain't nuttin but a ugly, big-mouf, black nigger. I done see you write, you know, 'cause you writ me a valentine once, you 'member. You cyahs pen an' ink 'roun' wid you, jes like muh ole marster used to do when he went to court. You got 'em in yo' pocket now, an' now I warn you to write."

Pettigrew by this time was ready to promise anything. "I will," he said. "What you warn me to write? Who mus' I write to?"

"Well," said Andrew, pensively, "I warn you to write to de meetin'."

Pettigrew's eyes brightened; he saw escape in it.

Andrew saw it too. "I warn you to write it mighty good," he said. "Ef you don't, I's gwine to kill you right heah."

A little of Pettigrew's courage came back in the presence of Andrew's mildness, and he said, "Ef you wuz to kill me dey'd hang you."

"Dey don't hang 'stracted folks," said Andrew. "I done larnt dat at de 'sylum, an' you know you's de one dat tol' 'em I wuz 'stracted." He leaned down over him and peered into his face.

"I'll write," said Pettigrew, brokenly.

Andrew got out the ink, pen, and paper, and placed the book on Pettigrew's knee. "I's gwine cyah it to muh little Johnnie fust. He kin read writin' mighty good; jes ez good ez you kin," he added. "An' ef dey's anything wrong, er ef he cyarn't read it, I's gwine to let you starve to death right heah."

Pettigrew protested. "What you warn me to write?" he asked, feebly.

"Well," said Andrew, meditatively, "I warn you to write 'em what a nice, white, colored gent'man I is, jes like you done said to me heah, an' dat I ain't no mo' 'stracted den you is; an' I warn you to tell 'em dat you done had to go right back to de 'sylum, an' dat you done git de word fum Wash'n'ton dat dey's all to vote to-morrow fer muh young marse Johnnie, an' dat ef dey don't de word 'll come fum Wash'n'ton 'bout it. Kin you 'member dat?"

Pettigrew remained so long immersed in thought that Andrew said, suddenly rising:

"Nem mine; I don' b'lieve I warn dat anyways; I is a 'stracted nigger, an' I ruther burn you a little anyways." And he turned to the fire and pulled out a chunk again.

Pettigrew protested that he would write, and after a little his keeper replaced the chunk, and loosening his right arm, gave him his pen and book. He squatted by him, and held the inkstand in one hand and the blazing knot in the other as a torch.

"Begin by tellin' 'em what a nice gent'man I is," he said, following with his eye the slow tracing of the pen on the paper. Pettigrew wrote carefully.

"Now read it," said Andrew.

He read it, and it appeared to satisfy him.

"Dat's it," he said, approvingly. "Now tell 'em how you's got to go right back to de 'sylum. Now read it. Arn harh!" he said, nodding with satisfaction as it was read. "Now tell 'em how de word done come fum Wash'n'-

ton, an' dey mus' vote fer muh young marster, an' do ev'ything jes like I say." It was written.

"Now sign yo' name to it," he said, "an' 'dress it to de meetin', to Brer Johnson; 'cause I ain't no great han' at foldin'," he apologized. "But don' seal it," he said, with a sudden change of manner. "I gwine git muh little Johnnie to read it; he can seal it; an' ef dee's a word wrong in it," he said, leaning down and looking at it keenly, "I gwine to lef' you heah to starve to death. You 'member 'bout dat valentine?"

The explanation of his prisoner appeared to satisfy him, and he took the letter and started away.

"You ain' gwine to lef' me heah in dis place by myself, is you?" asked the captive, glancing around fearfully.

"Yaas; you'll have plenty of company," said Andrew, grimly. "Evil sperrits all aroun' heah, thick as dem bushy hyahs on yo' head; I sees 'em heah any time; two on 'em over yonder now, a-settin' upon dat tombstone grinnin' at you." He half turned, faced the tombstone, and taking off his hat, bowed politely. "Good-evenin', marster," he said. "Hope you's well dis evenin'. Dey ain' gwine hu't you till I come back," he added, reassuringly, to Pettigrew, "ef you keep right quiet; ef you don', dey'll roas' you right whar you settin'. I gwine to leab de fire heah fer 'em. Jes keep yo' eye on him good, marster, tell I come back," he said, with another bow to the tombstone. He examined the rope carefully, and turning, disappeared with his letter in his hat.

It was ten o'clock when he walked into the meeting at the church. At first, there was much excitement with some threats against him, but his coolness held them at bay. He walked up to the desk of the clerk, and with a sudden instinctive power of command, ordered him to call the meeting to order. It was done, and he produced his letter. It created consternation; but the writing was undoubted, and Andrew's story was too straightforward and earnest to be questioned. His sudden power of command, or something, placed the meeting under his control, and the leaders became his lieutenants.

The next day the precinct, under the lead of "Brer Johnson," to the astonishment of every one, and of no one more than himself, went solidly for Andrew's " Marse Johnnie," and he was elected.

It was claimed afterwards that this was a trick of certain politicians; but it is due to Pettigrew to say that he never united in the charge. He moved away from the county shortly afterwards, and he always declared that, whatever others might say, he *knew* that Andrew was " a 'stracted nigger."

"RASMUS"

Uncle Peter knew "Rasmus" as well as Rasmus knew him. That is saying a good deal, for Peter had worn out more whipstaffs over Rasmus's head than he could count. Indeed, this gives a very inadequate idea of the number of whipstaffs he had so broken, because, as he himself said, he " wa'n't no gre't hand at countin'," and when he was intrusted with money for the firm, which not infrequently happened, he used to say, on his return, as he spread it out on the table: " I reckon, Marse Henry, you had better count dat over. I 'spec' it is all dyah, 'cause I hold my hand out to him right study after he done count once, and looked mighty wise until he counted it over agin and said, ' Dat's right,' and den I come 'long; but I reckon you better count it over." The fact was that Uncle Peter had been "trying" Rasmus, and Rasmus had been trying Uncle Peter, ever since the day when "the old mule" (the mule that the firm had when Uncle Peter first came down from the country and demanded work of his "young master," his Marse Henry,) dropped dead in the shafts trying to back the dray up to the sidewalk. Uncle Peter had truly mourned for his mule. He allowed no one else to bury him, and he always talked of him with reminiscent affection, as if he had been a beloved member of his family; and when the firm took him down next day to look at a young mule in the pens near the stock-yards, he would not consent to the purchase of one until he had "tried" it. This was at least six years before the time herein referred to; but though the mule had been paid for within forty-eight hours, Uncle Peter never would admit that he was doing anything but "tryin'" her. This he told Rasmus herself at least a dozen times a day, in every conceivable tone between that of the most inviolable confidence and that of the direst menace. Occasionally he even told the firm so when his threats and blows floated in at the door of the warehouse and brought some one out to see what the trouble was, and to expostulate with him on his treatment of Rasmus. One day he actually marched solemnly into the office, and, hat in his hand, lodged a formal complaint against Rasmus, declaring that he had "done try her," and found she would not do.

"Why, what's the matter, Uncle Peter?" asked his employer and former master. "Doesn't she pull well?"

"Oh yes, suh, she pull enough. I 'ain't got no quoil wid Rasmus 'bout dat. She pull well as any mule I ever see, 'cep' de ole mule—I never see a mule pull like him—but she is de meanes' mule in de wull. She always pull de wrong way, and she won't back a step to save yo' life: she jes like a 'ooman. Ef you want her to go one way, she want to go turr torectly. Ef you want her to back, she want to go forrard; ef you want her to go forrard, she won't move till she done back over de house. I's done broke more whipstaffs over her head den I could cut on de ole place."

The old man was mollified with the statement that he had better go back and "try her a little longer;" and he went, muttering that he would "try her jest a little longer," and then if she didn't suit he would send her back "whar she come from."

"Uncle Peter," called his employer as he went out, " why do you call her Rasmus?"

He turned back. " I calls her Rasmus, Marse Henry, 'cause Rasmus is a mule-name, and I gwine knock her head off too ef she don't mind." He went out.

Nothing more was heard of the matter beyond Uncle Peter's customary threats coming in from the street. He and Rasmus got along in the same old friendly way, he ruining whipstaffs over Rasmus's head, and Rasmus ruining his temper, until one day a new member of the Society for the Prevention of Cruelty to Animals happened to come along just as Uncle Peter banged his whipstaff over Rasmus in the same old affectionate way. The next morning the old man was fined ten dollars in the police court, which his employers paid and deducted from his wages. A short time after that his employer, coming down the street, observed the dray standing at right angles to the sidewalk at some little distance from the curbstone, and Uncle Peter standing with his skid in his hand immediately in front of Rasmus, making violent feints of beating her over the head, but never really touching her. He

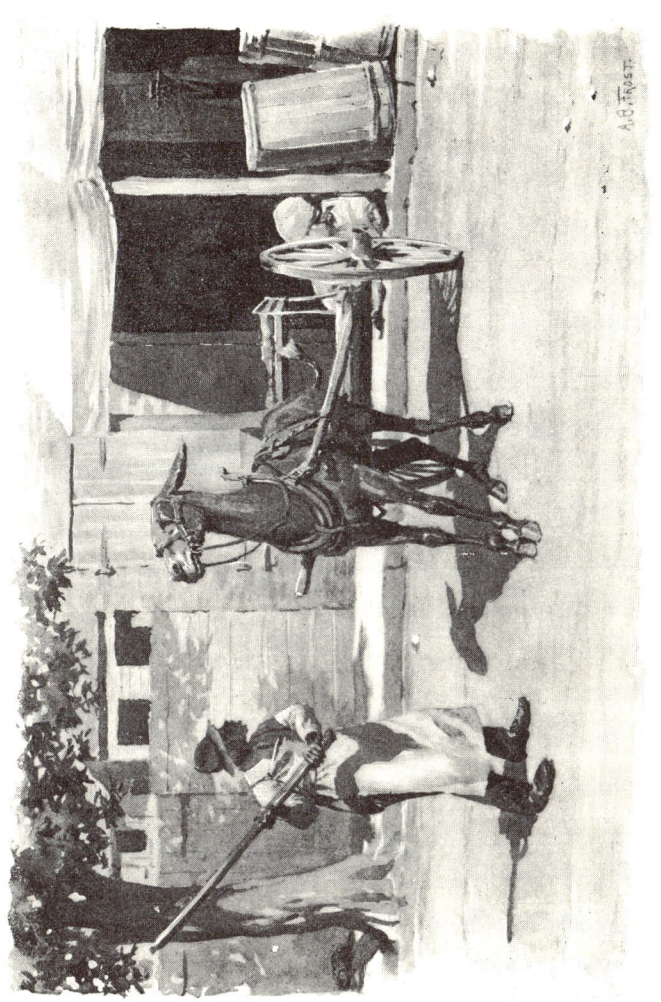

"'YOU KNOWS DEM CRUEL S'CIETY ANIMALS IS LOOKIN' ROUND'"

thought his failure to strike her was due to Rasmus's dodging. As he drew near, however, he heard Uncle Peter talking. With the skid uplifted in both hands as if ready to strike, he was saying: "Oh yes, you black Sattan, you! I know you! You done cost me ten dollars once, and you jest tryin' to git me agin. I knows you. You done had me down dere in de police cote 'bout hittin' you over your black head, and git ten dollars right out of my pocket, and you jest tryin' to make me hit you agin. But you ain't gwine do it, I tell you. You knows dem Cruel S'ciety Animals is lookin' 'round here, and you jest want me to pay you anurr ten dollars agin. I'd like to bust your black brains out, but I wouldn't tetch you to save your life. Back, fool! Don't you hear me?" He brought the skid down terrifically, as if he would smash the mule's head in, but stopped just short of touching her.

His employer, amused at his ire, said, "Uncle Peter, I reckon we had better sell that mule and get another one that will back."

The old fellow's countenance fell. "Sell her? Sell Rasmus? Nor, suh. Marse Henry, dat's de best mule in dis town. She got de debbel in her, dat's all. You lef her to me. I'll make her back. I'll breck her."

Just then Rasmus, as if she understood the whole situation, quietly backed up against the curbing, and calmly drooping her head, let her ears fall forward, and peacefully shut her eyes.

Peter went around and replaced the skid, and as his master went into the door he heard him saying to Rasmus: "Yes, you black Sattan, you better had back. You heah what he says? I's de only one done save you. Nem mind; next time he want to sell you I'm gwine to let you go. He'd sell you long ago ef I'd let him. I jest gwine to try you a little longer. I boun' den you will find somebody dat 'll make you back, and den you'll know how good I wuz to you."

HER SYMPATHETIC EDITOR

The editor sat in his sanctum (the name for all places where that particular species of animal sits, and which is so called because it is sacred to every soul who can scribble a line except the editor himself). The implements of his craft lay all about him—scissors, paste-pot, litter, waste-basket, and all. A pile of letters was before him, interspersed with MSS. in that intricacy of arrangement which only editors understand, and which to the ordinary mortal would be the superlative of disorder.

His associate sat at a side desk glancing over MSS., and placing them in piles for future examination, further consideration, or return, the second pile being the smallest, and the last much the largest. Odes to Spring, Summer, Autumn, and Winter, to the Snow, the Frost, to Rain, Hail, and Sunshine, had been tossed on the return pile with perfect impartiality; papers on George Washington, on the Treefrog, on the Punic Wars, the Tariff, Napoleon Bonaparte, and Noah's Ark, had experienced the same commendable exemption from prejudice.

Finally the associate editor said, " Well, here is a letter." He read a few sentences, and passed the letter across to his chief. " Did you read it?"

" No. It's ten pages, and I have only one lifetime—" exclaimed the other.

" I knew it," said the associate, with a virtuous air, interrupting the further protest. " But it's a woman, and she says that she is pining for intellectual companionship."

" For the intellectual companionship of a young magazine editor," cut in the editor, in his turn, casting his eyes down the closely written and crossed pages to find the name. " Where the mischief is it ? Here, find it if you can." He tossed the letter back to his associate. " I'll wager that she is a tall and vinegary dame who lets her husband eat sour bread and her children wear undarned stockings, while she writes poems on 'The Eternal Adolescence of the Infinite.' By-the-way, where is the poem?"

" I bet she is not; she is a young, fresh, enthusiastic girl with large blue eyes and a rose-leaf skin, and she teaches school and supports a widowed mother and two little sisters, and sends her younger brother to college, and he bullies her, and she writes poems of Lilacs and the Sunset," said her champion, raking over the pile of "Further consideration" papers. "What's the name?" he asked.

"'J. L. Speritt,' as well as I can make it out," said the senior.

"But where is the poem?" said his associate.

"Isn't this it?" asked the editor, looking into the waste-basket and picking up a good-sized MS. rolled together as tightly as paper can be rolled. The younger man took it.

"Yes, this does look like the same hand. It must have fallen into the basket."

"It is written on both sides, and does not appear to have any postage enclosed for its return. Perhaps that was the reason it was thrown there."

"Perhaps," said the associate. "You might at least have taken the trouble to read it, for the poor young thing will expect an answer anyhow. I wouldn't be as hard-hearted and unsympathetic as you for anything; and besides, I have no doubt the poem is at least up to the average."

"I do not deny that. Let's see. Read a little of it if you can. What is it called?"

The champion began: "'Ode to—' What is this?"

"Sour Bread?" suggested his friend.

"Not at all. 'To—to'—"

"The Lilac at Sunset?"

"No. 'To—My Affinity.'"

"Infinity — the Adolescence of Infinity. I told you that was it."

"No; it's 'Affinity.'"

"Well, that supports the sour-bread theory, anyhow. Go ahead."

The associate persevered:

"'Oh, thou who dwellest from me far,
    Through all the lonely, languorous hours
  Thou art to me a shining star
    'Mid amaranthine bowers.'"

A shade passed over the reader's face as his senior cut his eye around at him, and he furtively felt to see how many stanzas there were.

"How many pages are there? What do you think we ought to pay for that?"

"Well, it is not very— But she's young," said the associate. He let the paper go, and it sprang together like a coiled wire.

"It strikes me as quite 'very,'" said the editor; "but you are the poet's friend, and you can do as you like."

"Well," said the younger, after a pause, "I am sincerely sorry for the poor soul, and I'll take it. We need not publish it."

"All right," said the editor; "but it would be a great deal better to write frankly and tell her the thing's rot, and that she'd better darn her children's stockings and see that the bread is sweet."

He went back to his work, and the associate editor returned to his, writing among his first letters one to the authoress of the "Ode to My Affinity." In it he enclosed a check—not a very large one—and said as little as he could about the poem, which he pitched into a drawer.

The incident was forgotten until the next month, when, a few days after the appearance of the magazine, the mail brought a letter of nineteen pages from the authoress, expressing her disappointment that her Ode had not appeared, and asserting in vigorous language her opinion of its superiority to several poems which had been published. The associate editor read this letter first, and slipped it covertly out of the way, with a side look at his senior. He started to write a reply, stating that magazines were made up several months before their issue; but he thought better of it, and took no notice of the letter. During the next month and the next came other letters, each longer and more upbraiding than its predecessor, the last openly declaring the writer's opinion that only malicious jealousy or a more dishonest motive could instigate such treatment, which she characterized as "outrageous" and "ungentlemanly."

The associate had just read this letter, and was scratching his head over it, when the editor, looking up, caught his woe-begone expression.

"What is it—a raking from the poetess?" he asked, maliciously.

"Well, yes, that's just what it is," said the associate.

Just at that moment voices were heard in the outer office—the voice of the young lady clerk who had a desk there, and a strange and higher voice, which was doing most of the speaking.

"Well, I don't want to talk to any young woman; I did not come here for that. I've got five children older than you. I want to see the editor, and I am going to." The next instant she bounced into the door, a sharp little arrow-faced woman, with a keen, thin nose, thin lips, and small, black, beady eyes, above which was a fringe of dark hair plastered down as stiff as lacquered tin. She carried a black bag in one hand and a red fan in the other, which she brandished as if it were a weapon.

"Which is the poetry - editor? Or maybe you are both the *gen*tlemen!" (with a strong sarcastic emphasis on the first syllable). "Well, I have come to know what you have done with that poem I sent you months ago, and which you accepted, and have suppressed." She seated herself sharply, and threw out her fan with a whir like a lasso.

The associate editor, seeing her intention to take possession without an invitation, said,

"Madam, will you take a seat?" She glared at him witheringly, conveying plainly her declaration that she did not need his permission to do so.

"Well, what have you done with my poem?" she asked, with cold severity, as Draco might have asked of some luckless victim who stood a self-confessed thief.

"Madam, that is the poetry editor," said the chief, with a twinkle in his eye.

"Ah!" She gave a sharp half-wheel towards the associate. "Well, I'm glad to find the right person. And my name is not Speritt, nor Spirit, nor Brandy, nor anything like it, though I have no doubt you are quite familiar with all those names. My name is Spinks, Mrs. Spinks, and a very good respectable name it is, too, even if it is not as aristocratic as the one I gave up to take it, which was Rowlings —though, no doubt, you never heard of it, as you must be giving up all your time to reading the stuff you publish, which is enough to make any one sick who has a grain of the divine afflatus in her soul—being second-cousin once removed to Colonel Spangles, if you ever heard of him, as no doubt you are ready

"WHICH IS THE EDITOR?"

enough to claim you have, being on the Governor's staff for three years, till he took the fever and died, leaving one of the biggest fortunes in the State, and six children, and a widow, who gives herself as many airs as if she wa'n't old Sam Malony's daughter that kept the bar at Twenty-second Street. Well, I want to tell you that I know my rights, and I mean to have them. If Mr. Spinks had had a grain of manhood in him he'd have come down here and had that poem published in the very next number of the magazine after you suppressed it; but he hasn't. But I have, and I've consulted a lawyer, and he says it's a clear case, and I can get damages, and big damages at that, and I'm going to, and he's one of the best lawyers in the country, and a great friend of mine. What have you done with it?"

She paused for breath in sheer exhaustion.

The associate editor was speechless; but the chief came to his rescue. He said, calmly:

"Madam, we shall not be able to publish your poem. It was accepted under a mistake, and we will return it to you."

Her countenance fell.

"What!" she began; but he was too quick for her. He saw his advantage.

"The poetry editor has it and will return it to you, and you can keep the money we sent you in payment for the time we have had possession of it."

She rose.

"Well, I am glad to get it back on any terms. If I were not too much of a lady ever to be able to quarrel, I should give you a piece of my mind about it; but I never could quarrel."

"No, madam; your forte is poetry," said the associate editor, mildly, handing her the MS. roll, which he had got from its pigeon-hole.

"Thank you, I don't want any compliments from you, sir," she said, as she seized the paper and, unrolling it, looked over it page by page to see if any of it had been abstracted. Then she turned to the editor: "Good-morning, sir. I know a gentleman when I see him" (turning her head, with nose in the air, towards the associate).

She sailed out with her fan clutched in her

hand. The editor-in-chief, turning to his desk, began to murmur,

> " Thou art to me a shining star
> 'Mid amaranthine bowers,"

when the associate said: "The bread was sour, after all, wasn't it?"

HE KNEW WHAT WAS DUE TO THE COURT

HE was one of the characters about the town when I first knew it, and though I did not at the time know his history, and could not now avouch my witnesses, I somehow took it in from the city at large. He was not exactly a vagabond, for he had a house—a brick house at that, though a little one, and one of the oldest and most dilapidated in the town; and there was a garden beside it, though it was nothing more than a tangle of bushes, weeds, and briers, and no paling was left to the old enclosure. He was not exactly a drunkard in the police parlance, for though he was often full, he generally got home at some hour of the night, however drunk he might be, and he rarely got into the police court. (It may be doubted if a man can be a vagabond, however drunken and disreputable he may be, if he has a house of his own to which he can retire at will, and a garden, however grown up and unenclosed, in which he can wander when he chooses.)

If he was not a vagabond, however, it was a shadowy wall which withheld him from being one; and if he was not a drunkard, the line which divided him from it was impalpable. He was of a family which once owned a considerable part of the land on which the town was built. Other members of the family had got rich thereby, but he had grown poorer and poorer. He belonged to a past age, and was at loggerheads with everything new. He was a privileged character. He abused everybody, but nobody minded him. If he said a biting thing, every one laughed; if he got drunk, some one carried him home and poked him inside of his broken door; if he got angry, some one took his stick from him till he became quiet. He was known universally as "Old Jerry." How he lived was not absolutely known. No one would have dared to offer to give him anything.

He had been sheriff at one time—a fact of which he was very proud. He had owned then not only the old house and its torn garden, but the ground on both sides of it where the two large factories, owned by a nephew and namesake of his, a somewhat pompous gentleman, had since gone up. At least, he claimed to have owned this ground, though the courts had decided otherwise. People said generally that whiskey and dissipation had ruined him; he said the man who owned the factories on either side of him, and the rascality of the world at large, had done so, and he expended every resource at his command in annoying him. He had long since encumbered the remnant of his property, the old house and garden, in fighting him, and when he lost the suits he consoled himself by devoting hours a day to vilifying him wherever he could get a hearer to listen, which was not difficult. He always treated me with distinguished politeness, though I was counsel against him. He was paralyzed at this time, and could just shuffle along with his hook-handled stick; but his command of language was by no means as limited as his command of his limbs, and he used to curse his nephew with a lavishness which would have put Arnulphus to the blush. He even applied to court to change his rela-

"HE WAS NOT EXACTLY A VAGABOND"

tive's name, claiming that he had no right to it; and when that was refused, threatened to change his own name, that it might not remain the same with his.

At length his kinsman's patience gave way; the application to court to change his name was the last feather, and matters culminated. He applied for a writ of lunacy, and Old Jerry was brought up before three justices to be examined. I was counsel. We appeared before the magistrates in the justices' room in a corner of the old court-house looking out over the old part of the town, where the fashionable residences had been years before when the town was a village, but which was now almost covered by tall factories, with their blank walls and high chimneys. Almost the only break among them was the gap immediately facing the window, where a dingy little old house, with dormer-windows and a broken porch, was set back in an unfenced yard filled with bushes, and half hidden by two or three scraggy old trees, which leaned above it as if to rest on it as much as to shelter it.

When we arrived Old Jerry was already there in charge of the deputy sheriff. He was dressed in a clean shirt which showed marks of darning, and his long gray beard gave him a distinguished air. I had fallen in with the three magistrates and one of the examining physicians just outside the door, and the other doctor who had been summoned soon arrived. As we entered, Old Jerry tried to rise. The officer said he need not get up; but he shuffled to his feet, and made a profound bow to the magistrates, remaining standing until they had all taken their seats, when he tremulously resumed his. He never looked at his nephew, though his manner showed hostility in every fibre of his frame.

"Do you think I do not know what is due to a court, sir? I was sheriff before you were born," he said to the officer, who half smiled and said nothing. "Yes, sir, no deputy either —High Sheriff, who made deputies, sir." The officer still said nothing, and the next moment the old fellow apologized to him, declaring that he had always treated him like a gentleman. "Which is more than I can say for every one in this room," he added.

There was a brief consultation among the magistrates, and then the one who had issued the writ said that they would begin the inquiry. The papers were examined and found in form, and then the two doctors were called upon to testify. The evidence was all one way, and was pretty clear. Old Jerry had persistently refused for years to sell his old house or garden, and had let bushes grow on land worth five dollars a square foot till it was all eaten up. He had pursued his nephew with extraordinary virulence. There were, besides, a great many other curious things. This proved something, certainly; the doctors thought, insanity. Old Jerry sat scornfully silent till they had both testified. This ended the evidence. The presiding justice asked him if he wished to say anything. He said no, not there—he should appeal; but a moment afterwards, as they were writing out the committal, he said, suddenly, " There is one infamous rascal in this room." Everybody looked up. " I don t refer to you, your Worship, or you, or you, sir," to one justice after the other, very blandly. " I know too well what is due to the court; and "—turning and looking at me very doubtfully—" I don't mean you, either, sir: I knew your father, and he was a gentleman. I know you've been trying to help rob me of my house all these years, but I don't blame you; that's your business that you are paid for. And I don't mean you, or you," addressing the doctors: " if I were speaking of fools, I might not be able to overlook you. I don't mean you, Mr. Sheriff, and " —more briskly—" I don't mean myself." He sat back and looked straight ahead of him, while his relative shifted uncomfortably in his chair and tried to look unconcerned.

The committal was made out and delivered to the officer, who, with some evident concern, beckoned to him, on which he rose and went shuffling out, stopping at the door to make a profound bow to the court to which he knew so well what was due.

A few days later I met the old fellow shuffling along on the street, and I suppose I showed some surprise in my face, for he stopped and spoke to me.

" I'm back, you see," he said, cheerfully.

" Yes; how is it ?"

" Well, you see," he said, " when I got to the asylum where that rascal got me sent the board was in session, and I knew most of them, and their fathers before them; and they asked me what I was doing there, and I made a clean breast of the whole thing—all about that scoundrel who has been robbing me, and you, and those two other fools, and all; and that I had a damned sight more sense than all of you put together; and they said they knew you all, and that I was right."

He shambled off.

HER GREAT-GRANDMOTHER'S GHOST

WE had been talking of ghosts, in which my old mammy had taught me to believe.

"I was not a particle superstitious in my early days, but I had a singular experience once," she said, in her calm, soft voice. "You know my people all came from Gloucester County, and the old family-place is there. It was too expensive to keep up after the war, the house being one of the large, old-fashioned, colonial brick mansions, and my father having no taste for country life (or rather, perhaps, I should say he was not able to support the family and educate us in the country after the neighborhood was broken up). So he removed first to a city in Virginia, and then to New York. He never would sell the place, but at every sacrifice kept it just as it was, with the old furniture and all in it, renting some of the fields out, and getting a neighbor to look after it, as well as to take care of Uncle Benny, the old butler, who still lived. He always talked of going back there, and used to tell us stories of it in his childhood, when the large grounds were kept up, and the house was constantly full of visitors. I got thus an accurate idea of the house, except that I always pictured it as being of immense size, and I knew every room and crevice in it as well as if I had been brought up there, instead of never having seen it since I left it at three years old. I knew as well as if I had lived there the old garret where the trunks and chests used to stand; the wide stairway, with the landings and the turned balusters; the big hall, with its settle around the large fireplace; and the drawing-rooms, with the straight-backed chairs, and the long mirrors coming down to the floor, and the old family portraits on the walls, from one of which the faded lady with the brown ringlets and the black dress used to come down on summer evenings and rock in the big rosewood rocking-chair, so that every one could hear her all over the house. She was the daughter of my father's great-grandfather, and having lost her husband soon after her marriage, came home to live with her father.

When he died, which was not long afterwards, she lived with her little boy all alone in the house, and used to spend hours by herself in the drawing-room, sitting in the rocking-chair, weeping or looking vacantly before her. Her servants used to take her orders from her there. Finally she was induced to leave, and went away to visit some relatives; but one day when the old butler went into the parlor she was sitting in her rocking-chair as usual, only paler than ever. She did not seem to know him, and asked who he was, and then sent him to look for her carriage, saying she was going away. There was no carriage in sight, nor had any been seen to drive up, and when he went back she was dead in her chair. How she got there no one knew. My father always said I looked like her.

"My father died suddenly, you know, without ever having fulfilled his wish to go back there to end his days. I was seized immediately with an irresistible desire to see the place, and I wrote to his old friend and neighbor that I should come down on a particular day to see it. He wrote me that he would be delighted to see me, and would meet me at the wharf some miles off. The impulse to go, however, was so strong that I could not wait till the day I had appointed; so I packed up and set out at once. I thus arrived at the wharf two or three days before I was expected, and there was no one to meet me. The man who kept the little store there, however, learning where I was going, kindly agreed to send me over to my destination, and called a boy to hitch a horse to a buggy; and when I asked him what I should pay him, declined to receive pay, saying that he was in my father's company during the war, and never charged neighbors anything, and the horse wasn't doing anything, anyhow.

"I however insisted on paying something, and he finally named a price which was so low that I, who was used to city charges, felt all day as if I had robbed him. The hitching up of the horse took some time, but I did not mind it, for my new friend said dinner was ready, and I must come over and get some. I saw that he wanted me, and I went over to the little house back in a yard behind the store. There I was received by a motherly woman, who made me welcome, and was set down to a plain but substantial dinner. My hosts seemed to know all about the gentleman to whose house I was going, and assured me that he would be very glad to see me. I asked them if they had ever been to the old place. The man said he had, and that it had been a fine place once. The woman gave a little half-nervous laugh. 'I 'ain' ever been there,' she said, 'and I don't want to go.' I asked her why. 'Too many ghosts there,' she laughed, as if half ashamed of her superstition. Her husband pooh-poohed it, but she stuck to her point. 'They say that old lady can be seen there any time in broad daylight, and that old negro too; and they'd be sure to be there now the place has been shut up so long.' I said that I was not afraid of ghosts.

"In a short time I was on the way in a little rickety, high-pitched buggy, which made as much noise as a coach, with my host's son, Tommy, a sleepy-looking, shock-headed boy of fourteen, as my driver. I found that Tommy did not believe in ghosts; but he admitted that he did not like graveyards at night, though he did not mind them in the day, and he didn't care to go around old deserted houses alone even in the daytime. He had never been to our old place, and would not care to go by himself, though he would not admit that he was afraid to do so.

"We had been on the road over an hour, most of the time driving through what seemed to me an unbroken forest, with only a cabin now and then to break the monotony, though Tommy occasionally pointed to dim roads going off into the woods, and indicated them as Mrs. So-and-So's place. Presently, he pointed to a road almost grown up. 'That's your place,' he said. Suddenly an irresistible impulse seized me, and I asked him if he would mind going in there with me. He said not, though he was evidently surprised and a little startled; and as we drove along the old road, washed into gullies and grown up in weeds, he intimated that we should probably see the lady in black and her old negro. We had to go up and down several hills, though none very high, and cross one or two fields which were in a partial state of cultivation, which he said was done by renters. Then we came to the last hill, on which the house stood.

"The grounds were really quite extensive, or had been, for the fence around the house and yard had once enclosed several acres. It was now all broken down, and many of the trees were gone, so that the old house, standing up stark in the hot sunlight, looked gaunt and bare. I remembered that my father had had a tenant at one time in the yard, and that he had turned him off because he cut down so many of the yard trees.

"The grass was very short, which my companion explained by stating that the house field was rented as a pasture, and the sheep and cows liked to graze around an old house spot. 'That's the graveyard,' he said, pointing to a group of tombstones, some still standing, and others lying about, off to one side under a clump of trees which I knew had once been in the garden. I made him drive across the grass to it, but did not get out there. A small flock of sheep were lying down among the old tombs. The place did not appear very terrifying, and as I wished to be left to wander about quite alone, I told my companion that he could drive back down the road a few hundred yards and wait for me. He seemed to be relieved, for he had hardly taken his eyes from the old door since we drove up, as if he momentarily expected the ghostly lady and her sable butler to walk out on us, and he accepted my proposal with alacrity, though he evidently regarded me as demented. He drove over towards the house, and I sprang out, and he rattled off across the grass and was soon out of sight, though for some little time I could hear his vehicle. I stood and gazed at the house with a strange feeling. It filled me with emotion; I was fascinated by it. Here was where my father was born, and had lived, and where I was born, the last of my branch of the family. The silence and softness of the warm summer afternoon settled down about me, and I walked about on the short grass under the trees almost as if I were in a trance. The sound of a cat-bird from time to time in a clump of locust-bushes seemed to fill all the quiet air, and when it ceased the stillness was almost painful; the sunlight glistened in wavering billows above the ground. I observed that several of the window-shutters were open —blown back, I judged, in some wind. I went up the steps and walked to the front door;

but it was fastened. I put my eye close to the cobweb-filled windows beside the door and peeped in. I could see the wide hall dimly lighted through the large fan-shaped transom over the door. The big fireplace had the old brass andirons in it, and the settle beside it, and there were several old chairs ranged back along the walls. I could see the end of the wide staircase where it came down.

"I went around and tried a door at the side, and found it either unlocked or so shrunken that the bolt did not catch, and I could push it open. This let me into a narrow passageway which I knew led into the hall; so, leaving the door slightly ajar, I went in. The place was oppressively close, and I went over to the front door to try to open it, instinctively stepping softly to prevent any sound of my footsteps. It was fastened by a bar across, and I found it so difficult to undo that I let it alone, and went to the door of the drawing-room or parlor on the right, one window-shutter of which I knew had blown open.

"I found the door unlocked, and entered. The room was large and high-pitched, and filled with old-fashioned, stiff, black furniture.

A half-dozen old portraits, more or less faded, hung on the walls in frames dim with age and neglect. At the windows hung old-fashioned, yellow, brocaded satin curtains very much worn, and two long pier-glasses in gilt frames reached from the floor almost to the ceiling, and repeated everything in the room. It was too dim to see much, so I put back a curtain to let in a little more light—it was thick with dust—and opened the window to get the air. Among the pictures the most striking one was that of a lady in deep black which hung over the old mantel-piece. I knew at once that she was my ghostly great-grandmother; but I was struck by two things: she was not half as old as I had always imagined her to be; indeed, hardly more than a girl, and even in the dim light I could see the resemblance to myself. This picture fascinated me. Whichever way I turned, those large melancholy eyes followed me, until I forgot everything else and could look only at them. The light was not good on it where it hung, and I climbed upon a chair and tried to take the picture down to place it in a better light; as I did so, the cord, rotted with age, gave way, and it came near falling. I caught it, however, and, stepping down, set it on a chair against the wall opposite the window, and pulling up a large rocking-chair, took my seat where I could see it well. As I sat there a strange feeling came over me. To think that I, sitting alone in that old house, was the last survivor of my family. Suddenly I felt a singular nearness to the woman in the frame before me. Of all who had lived there only two could come back—for, at least, she could come back to me, if only in imagination. She, too, had suffered; she, too, had sat there in her loneliness, where I sat now in mine. If I might but die there in that chair, as she had died, and be at rest! How long I sat there I do not know, but I seemed in a little while to have changed places with the woman in the chair; she was in the rocking-chair and I was in that by the wall.

"I became gradually conscious of a presence. I opened my eyes, and they fell on the long mirror to my right. In it I saw through the open door a man — an old negro man he seemed, though the shadow of the door on his face prevented my seeing him plainly. He wore a

"I BECAME GRADUALLY CONSCIOUS OF A PRESENCE"

curious-looking old beaver hat, and had a very serious expression on his face. His hand was on the knob, and he pushed the door noiselessly wider open as if to enter. At sight of me he stopped short, with a startled look on his face, and the next moment took off his hat and bowed low. 'Your sarvent, mistis,' he said, in a low voice. I was afraid to move. Was he a burglar or what? I tried to speak, but my throat and tongue were dry, and though I made a motion with my lips, there was no sound. I did not dare to take my eyes from the mirror. Presently, with an effort, I said, without moving, 'What do you want?' 'I am the butler, ma'am,' he said, with another low bow, his voice sounding very far away. 'Do you live here?' 'Yes, ma'am; dat is, I did live heah,' he said, with some hesitation. Thinking that if he had any malicious intention it might be well to let him know that I had a companion not far off, I said, as quietly as I could, 'It is time for me to go. Do you see my vehicle out there?' He seemed to bow. I turned quickly towards the door; but the door was shut. For the first time my nerves seemed shaken. What was he? After a moment's hesitation I roused myself and came out into the hall. It was empty. I made my way out by the same door by which I had entered. It stood slightly ajar as I had left it. In the sunlight my courage revived, and I went over to the old graveyard where the sheep lay in the sunshine and let me walk among them, only one or two jumping up and running off quickly a few paces, sneezing, with their noses to the ground. The cat-bird still sang in the clump of bushes among the tombs. Of course the one tomb which interested me more than all the others was that of my great-grandmother. It lay behind the bushes in which the cat-bird sang. She had died at the age of twenty-two, just my age then. A sheep-path led through a break in the fence out towards the road, and I took it and passed out that way. I found my driver almost in a fit over my long absence. He was sure that I had been caught by a ghost. I did not tell him what I had seen.

" On my arrival my host received me with great cordiality, and offered to drive me over to the old place that evening; but the hot sun had given me a headache. Old Uncle Benny was even more delighted to see me. He appeared almost startled at my looks.

"'Lord, master! You is like old mistis,' he exclaimed. 'Am I? Like my grandmother?' 'Norm; like you' pa's grandma—like dat one whar hang on de wall, an' walk all 'bout dyah, and come down and set in her big cheer in de parlor.' 'But you never saw her?' I said. ''Ain't I? Yes, 'm! I is, too. Done see her and talk to her too. You know my granddaddy he wuz de butler dyah in her time, jes like I wuz in you' pa's time, an' dee say I is jes like him; maybe dat's de reason she so frien'ly to me. I done see her right in broad daylight; I see her settin' in her big cheer, an' I see her when she come out an' tuck her kerrige to drive back to the graveyard. You know she so proud she have her kerrige even to drive herself from de graveyard to de house, and you is jes like her.' I said, 'Yes, my father always said I was like her.'"

RACHEL'S LOVERS

Rachel was as black as a crow, or, more poetically, as a sloe, but this did not prevent her from being a belle on the plantation; and though she had reached the mature age of twenty without taking a husband, it was not for want of offers, for she had had many. She was, indeed, the belle of the plantation; but she was also the flirt, and more than the usual number of the young bucks had endeavored to secure her without success. Finally it was supposed that Stable-Dick had won the prize and captured the sable nymph's coy affections, and the other lovers fell back. Dick was a strapping young fellow, with shoulders almost as broad as his stable-door, and was as black as Rachel herself. He had been her adorer ever since she was twelve years old, and Jacob never served her historical namesake more faithfully or joyfully than Dick did this ebon damsel. On St. Valentine's Day he

had for many years gotten his young master
Charlie (several years his junior) to write her
valentines, until they had utilized all the verses
in the category of scalloped missives, with
many of their own invention, which were more
original than poetic; at Christmas he had, with
unwavering loyalty, given her presents which
took all of the little tips he had received from
gentlemen whose horses he had taken during
the preceding months, and had requested her
to "accept his company" at the Christmas parties with unvarying fidelity, taking her customary refusal with as much meekness as he
took her occasional acquiescence with joy.
Thus, when Rachel finally smiled on him, and
one year, along towards the fall, began to accept his attentions, there was a general indorsement of her action on the plantation which was
akin to sentiment. Rachel herself felt the influence of it enough to openly encourage Dick,
and the wedding began to be talked about as
one of the events which were to make Christmas notable. Dick was already in the sixth
heaven, and was getting ready to climb into
the seventh, when a bar was placed across the
entrance. On the plantation there was one

of the characters which were almost always found on large plantations—an old darky who was always ready to shirk his duty, and to live, so to speak, by his wits, evading both his work and the other regulations of the plantation. He was generally a wag and occasionally something of a wit; or, failing this rare possession, he made good his position by a certain assurance which might take the form of grandness of manner or of mere impudence. Uncle Isaac was of the latter class. He had no wit; he was a drunkard, a liar, and a shirker; but he possessed a certain Chesterfieldian manner, copied from that of his old master, and so notably like it that it gave him an air of distinction which no woman on the place seemed able to resist, and which, when reenforced by constant reference to former companionship with his master, and to a certain blue coat with brass buttons which his master had once given him, impressed even the men. He was, moreover, something of an exhorter; not a preacher exactly, for he was far too fond of drink to enable him to shine in that rôle; but he supported acceptably that of exhorter, and his exhortations were the more impressive in that, whatever his life was, he was a most sincere believer in a personal Satan, with the most realistic accompaniments of fork, fire, and brimstone. Perhaps it was the fact of the former companionship with his old master which gained the old man indulgence from his "young master" (Charlie's father), and made him shut his eyes to infractions of the plantation law which would have got any other person on it into trouble.

Isaac had already had four wives, two of whom had departed in what is known as "the ordinary course of nature," their exit certainly facilitated if not caused by his treatment, and the other two of whom had departed in a different course, having left him because they were unable to stand his whippings, which were said to be not only frequent, but tremendous. This did not, however, at all impair Uncle Isaac's popularity with the sex, and his last wife had barely been borne from his cabin when the old man was a declared lover of Rachel, as well as of one or two less popular damsels, urging as his excuse for such promptness that text of Scripture which declares that it is not good for man to be alone.

In fact, the old fellow was notably afraid to be by himself, believing firmly that he was in danger of being carried off bodily by the fiend unless he had some living thing with him. He was accustomed to fortify himself during his periodical terms of widowerhood with a cat. The presence of a cat he believed to bring good-luck. "When cat woan' notice rat, den look out," he used to say. Whether it was that the idea of proving successful where four women had already failed, or whether it was the eclipsing of Molly and Betty; whether it was the magnificent airs and grandiloquent speech of old Isaac, or whether it was only the natural perversity of her sex that decided Rachel need not be discussed; but the October Sunday that Uncle Isaac appeared at the big baptizing in his old master's blue coat and brass buttons, which he wore only when he was "setting up to" his several wives, and held his old umbrella over Rachel, decided the fate of poor Stable-Dick; and though Isaac, after a most impressive exhortation, got so full that he fell down and broke his umbrella, and Rachel had to hold the now damaged article over him instead of his holding it over her, she incontinently accepted him and sent poor Dick adrift. She even went so far as to agree to marry the old fellow without waiting for Christmas, but, fortunately for Dick, their master interposed, and declared that he would not permit Isaac to maltreat any more wives, and would not consent to his marrying until he had reformed, and had proved his sincerity by his abstinence for a certain period. This period he at first fixed at six months, but upon the joint application of both Isaac and Rachel he agreed to reduce it to less than three, and set Christmas Eve as the final limit.

Perhaps the master thought that in this case two months were as good as six, and that Isaac would no more hold out that time than he would an eternity. At least, every one else thought so, except Dick; but Dick surrendered himself to despair. He moped around in the blackness of gloom, dividing his time between consigning the entire female sex of the African race to the lowest depths of perdition, and trying to get the faithless Rachel to give him even the smallest share of her thought. Finally, he went so far as to apply to his master and ask to be sold in the South. This was serious enough to call for the intervention of authority. The next thing might be a runaway, or even suicide, and Dick was told that if Isaac did not hold out, no further coquetting on Rachel's part would be allowed, and she should become his bride. Rachel also was notified, and simply giggled over this disposal of her freedom. This did not help her unhappy adorer, who was not comforted even by his young master Charlie's sympathetic assurance that Isaac would never hold out. " That ole drunk fool 'll hold out jest out o' pure cussedness," said he. It did, indeed, look as if Dick's apprehension was well-founded, and as week after week went by, Dick's spirits and those of his young master and ally sank. Charlie tried to secure his father's assistance in the cause, but was told that his word had been given to both Rachel and Isaac, and must stand. If Rachel chose to make a fool of herself, it was her right as a woman. Rachel made the most of her opportunity, and flounced about and flouted poor Dick with the cruelty and arrogance of a much more advanced state of civilization. Two days before Christmas Eve Uncle Isaac got an indulgence. He " had to get ready to be married." He shut himself up in his house, and was, or seemed to be, getting it in readiness for his fifth bride. Rachel, too, occupied herself in getting ready, with her young mistress's assistance, and enjoyed the notoriety of her position as much as the most fashionable bride could have done. Stable-Dick confined himself to the stable, and bemoaned his fate into the sympathetic ear of his young master. At length it occurred to that astute ally to go and see what direct intercession with the triumphant rival might avail. He sought Isaac in his cabin and made known his mission, when he was received with so much scorn that he nearly burst into tears. The disappointment was too much.

"Uncle Isaac, you know you are three times as old as Rachel," he asserted, "and Dick is just the right age."

"Dat's so much de better," said the old man, with a guffaw. "I'll know how to manage her; 'ooman and chillern needs management; hit's jes like physic to 'em. I got de physic for her." He glanced up at a peg in the wall from which hung a large bunch of hickories, which rumor said he had often used during his earlier periods of matrimony on Rachel's predecessors. Some of the switches looked new enough to suggest replenishment.

Charlie's eye caught the direction of his, and he fired up. "I'm going to tell Rachel," he said. "You know you beat your other wives scandalously."

The old fellow looked at him angrily. "Dat's some lie o' dat black trundle-bed-trash nigger Stable-Dick," he said, scornfully. "I'll trick him if he fool wid me. I jes keep dem switches to whup my cat."

Charlie's last arrow was gone. His eyes filled with tears at the failure of his mission. "Uncle Isaac," he said, "if you'll give Rachel up I'll pay you."

He did not see the change in the old man's face, nor the shrewd look which crossed it. "How much you gwine gi' me?" he asked.

"Well, I've got a dollar and a half, and I'll get another dollar in my stocking Christmas morning." He paused to see if he had any other available assets.

"Is you got any ole umbrella you kin gi' me?" asked the trader for a wife.

"No-o; but I think I could get mamma

to give me one. There are several in the house."

"Well, I tell you what I'll do: if you'll go and git me de dollar an' a half right now, and 'll git me de best umbrella you kin, an' 'll promise me to gi' me your dollar Christmas mornin', I'll see 'bout it."

Charlie promised faithfully, and rushed away, too eager to carry out his part of the bargain to notice the other party's sharp look, or hear his gibe: "Yes, I gwine see 'bout it, an' dat's all I is gwine do."

A few minutes later Charlie returned with the dollar and a half, his entire available assets, and having deposited it, with a statement that he thought he could get the umbrella, rushed away to report to Dick the happy result of his mission.

Later that evening Charlie returned to the old man's cabin to learn his decision, but the cabin was locked, and a survey of it through the cat-hole revealed only Uncle Isaac's black cat "Torm" lying on the hearth before the fire, tied to an old plough-point, which was the old man's mode of insuring his continual presence.

A few hours later a figure in the darkness approached the cabin door with curiously unsteady steps. Something in a bag was slung over its shoulder. There was a long fumbling over the lock, and then the door opened, the figure disappeared inside, and the door was shut.

The next day Uncle Isaac did not appear. Charlie's most earnest appeals outside of the fastened door failed to bring any answer.

The cat-hole was stopped up, so that the interior of the room was beyond inspection. Charlie was running off to announce the old man's disappearance, when the smoke from the chimney caught his eye. All during the day he made repeated visits to the cabin, but neither hammering nor calling could elicit any response. At last, about dusk, his impatience became too strong, and he applied himself to making a "chink" through which he could see if Isaac were really inside. After a quarter of an hour he succeeded in making a good hole, and, stooping down, he peeped in. In another moment he was speeding breathless towards the place where he knew Dick was, and five minutes later that young Hercules was lying stretched out on the frozen ground, with his eye screwed to the hole Charlie's industry had made. What they saw inside was Uncle Isaac sitting in front of his fire as drunk as a lord, with a large jug between his wabbling knees.

The next minute Charlie was in Stable-Dick's arms, being whirled about at the risk of losing his head in the latter's joyful gyrations. There was a hasty and whispered colloquy, interrupted by Charlie's giggles as he unfolded some plan, and then the boy rushed off, followed by Dick, his big white teeth looking like rows of corn. When, a half-hour later, the two returned, Charlie had equipped himself with a long fishing-pole, a powder-horn, and one or two other articles: Dick had a ladder. They peeped in at the hole. Uncle Isaac still sat as they had left him, only drunker than before. He was fast asleep, and his old cat lay dozing nearer to the sinking fire. A noise roused the old fellow, and he sat up. His eye fell on his jug, and he lifted it unsteadily and took a drink from it. It seemed to revive him. "Whiskey tas'e mighty good when you been dry long time," he said. This reflection induced him to take another pull at the jug. Just then there was a sound as of some one climbing at the top of the chimney. "Hi! what dat?" muttered the old fellow, lowering his jug. His eye fell on his cat, and he stretched out his leg and stirred him up. "Heah, wake up, Tormy!" he said. "Nem mind; I gwine git mistis for you, and ef she don' treat you well, I gwine gi' her hickory."

The anticipation pleased the old fellow so much that he resorted again to his jug, and under its reviving influence be began to sing a snatch from a corn-shucking song:

> "I went down to Helltown,
> Found de deble chained down,
> Oh, Loo John! oh, Loo!
> I hitch' him to my horse-cart,
> And put him in a long trot,
> Oh, Loo John! oh, Loo!"

Just then a large brown rat floated down the chimney, and dropped close to Torm, who pounced upon it, but the next instant settled back to his nap. The rat caught the old man's eye, and he kicked the cat up again.

"Don't you see dat rat, fool?" he said. But

Torm was not interested. He never looked, and simply turned over on his other side.

"Well, dat's de curisomest thing I ever see," said Isaac. "Dat's a rat, sho'! but I 'ain' never see Tormy do dat away befo'. I's gwine to see ef dat's a rat." He took up his stick and leaned forward. But as he struck at it the rat disappeared up the chimney, and losing his balance, he fell forward on his face.

"Well, befo' de King!" he exclaimed, picking himself up. Just then the rat appeared again, swinging gently to and fro. "Dat rat look might'ly to me like he was flyin'," said Isaac, picking up the jug. Just then there was a spit of blue flame in the ashes, and Torm jumped to his feet. "Heah, le' me put dis thing down," said the old man. A noise on top of the chimney caught his ear. He started. "What dat? I done heah 'bout folks comin' down chimbley Christmas, but I 'ain' never liked it. Master, please don' come down heah," he called, in supplication, and began to chant a hymn as a sort of spell against the possible visitation. Just then the rat appeared again, and after hovering a few moments above the embers, lit close to the once more drowsy Torm. It was rather blacker than it had been, as if there were something like a black powder on its back. "I's gwine to see ef dat's a rat or a evil sperit," said Isaac, re-emboldened by his religious exercise. He leaned over and picked up from the corner a half-extinguished chunk, and bent towards the rat. As he did so he tipped the jug over. "Ef you's a rat, I'll know you," he said, grimly. He put the chunk on its back. The rat burst into blue sputtering flames, which danced up and down its back and sides, jumped into the ashes, and ran in zigzag lines about the hearth, until they reached the mouth of the overturned jug, when they wound up in a dazzling burst of flame, which threw coals and ashes all over the hearth.

Two seconds later Uncle Isaac had smashed out of his door, with his cat close behind him, every hair on its body which had not been singed off standing erect, and the rusty plough-point clattering along like a pursuing demon. He burst into the circle of revellers about the kitchen door like a wild man, swearing that the devil was after him.

"'EF YOU'S A RAT, I'LL KNOW YOU'"

The upshot of it all was that Rachel married Dick next night, in the gown which had been given her to wed Isaac, and giggled just as happily. Most people thought at first that Isaac had *delirium tremens*, but he always maintained that he saw the devil himself, and gave so circumstantial a description of him that it was quite convincing, and brought him so much renewed credit that Molly shortly afterwards married him, and, be it said, duly got the physic that he had prepared for Rachel.

JOHN'S WEDDING SUIT

John was a curious sort of fellow. He was one of the quietest-tempered men I ever knew; he had also more sentiment than most. When he was a boy his room was always littered up with what the other boys called "trash": odds and ends, broken whips, tops, knives, kites, dried grass, pressed flowers, etc., which no other boy cared about, but which were precious in John's eyes because they were associated with something which had given them a value to him. This top had been made by his father; this old knife had been won as a prize for going to a graveyard after dark; that book-mark was his little sister's first piece of embroidery, etc. He would stand an amount of teasing and chaffing which would have set any of the other boys at war; and then suddenly, when some little right had been invaded or some sentiment jarred, he would be a perfect fury. The other boys learned to know the signs, and would impose on him to a certain extent, but when his face began to grow pale and his hands to tremble, they stopped.

In time John became a doctor, and returned from college to practise medicine in his native town. He had a genius for physic, and his professors had urged him to go straight to a city; but he declined, and with his diplomas and prize cases of instruments went back to his little village, where he soon was practising on all the poor people and little girls' dogs in the place. Possibly the fact that his sweetheart, a pretty girl with whom he had been in love since his boyhood, lived there was one of the causes which brought him back. Anyhow, there he was, and when he was not at some sick-bed, or working over some lame beast, he was apt to be on the vine-covered veranda of her house or in its little plain parlor. If he was not at any of these places, he was sure to be poring over a book in his little office or playing with some child. None of these occupations, however, is very remunerative, and John was much busier than he was rich. Such a man is sure to be imposed on, and John was better liked than paid. If he ever collected a bill, the money went either to buy physic for some patient who could not afford it, or to get new books or new instruments. Thus John's library and instrument-case were a good deal better furnished than his wardrobe. He lived in a little room back of his office down on the principal street of the village, and was waited on by a boy whose only recommendation was that he was the son of one of John's father's old servants. A more worthless rascal could not be imagined—at least, such was the general opinion of John's friends. But John held on to him. They were about the same age, and had played together as boys, and this was sufficient. Cal (short for Caldicut) was a strapping young fellow about John's size, on which he prided himself, and of a dark gingerbread color. He was a bully, much feared among his set, who knew his strength, and the quickness with which he could whip out a razor as soon as he began to be worsted; a liar noted around town, and a thief, most people believed —some on general principles, others on more specific grounds. Few, however, ventured to suggest this to John, who was a fool about Cal, as many thought and some said. When

Cal was put in jail for cutting another darky at a dance, John used his utmost endeavors to get him off, and did succeed in getting him a very light punishment. He took him back as soon as he was out. Cal used to carry his notes to his sweetheart and wear his old clothes, which was pretty much all he did, for John's rooms were sadly neglected.

At length even John's mind waked up to this fact, and as Cal declared that he cleaned up every day, he set a trap for him, placing several papers on certain spots. There they were next day; but Cal, when reprimanded, explained that he dusted everything every night, but always put everything back just where he found it.

At length John's suit with his sweetheart prevailed, and she rewarded his years of constancy by finally "fixing the day." She had, in fact, always been in love with him, and had only waited so long because she knew she could marry him whenever she chose; and the torture she had inflicted on her lover was a species of cruelty which all her sex enjoy and, as many as dare, practise.

The town rejoiced in John's success and

joined in his happiness. He had the counsel of several of his friends as to his arrangements and outfit; for, as they said, unless some one looked after him, he would very probably forget his wedding-ring, if he did not forget his wedding-day, and be found, at the hour appointed for the ceremony, either gathering wild-flowers somewhere for his sweetheart, or setting off for a ten-mile drive to see some old woman who wanted him to cure her cat. A pretty little house had been secured, with more room outside on the vine-covered veranda than within its walls, and it was fitted up with what little the two young people could get together.

John went to the city at least a month ahead of time to get his wedding-suit. It was his first full evening suit, and he felt about it as a girl must feel about her first ball dress. He undid the parcel with his door locked, and a feeling as if it were a sacred relic; then tried it on gravely, and looked at himself solemnly. It fitted him exactly, and set off his strong figure well. But he did not think of this; he thought only of her. He took it off, and, folding it up again in the wrapping of tissue-paper, placed it in the box, and laid it away rever-

"HE LOOKED AT HIMSELF SOLEMNLY"

ently in his wardrobe, one side of which he cleared for its more fitting reception. He would wear it first when he claimed her for his wife. It was sacred in his eyes. Every day or two he locked his door, and, taking the suit out tenderly, laid it out and looked at it, but never put it on again, thinking to do her greater honor by wearing it first at her wedding, and dreaming dimly of laying it away afterwards in lavender and rose leaves.

The day before the wedding he set aside to clean up and settle his matters, which he had been delayed in doing by several very ill patients. They were still ill, so he set Cal to work and went off to see them. On his return he found little done and Cal absent. In a short while, however, Cal appeared. He would have met with a warm reception, but he prevented it by assuming a very mournful look. He spoke before John could say anything.

"Mr. Johnny"—he always used that term when he wanted to gain anything; it recalled old associations—"Mr. Johnny," he said, "I's had a mighty bad piece of luck hit me." He waited, and John looked at him. "I's done lost meh grandmother."

"Why, I thought you lost your grandmother two months ago!" said John. "You buried her, anyhow."

"Yes, suh. But this is my other grandmother."

John's face assumed a reminiscent expression. "Why, you lost one last winter too," he said, "and one— This is the fourth grandmother you have lost, to my certain knowledge."

"Yes, suh, dat's so. Dat ole man marry mo'n any other man I uver see in de wull," said Cal, reprobatingly. "She die' las' night, an' de funeral comes off dis evenin'; an' I thought I'd ax you to let me off dis evenin' to go to it."

He had spoken so rapidly that John had not had time to put in a question. He put one now, however. "When did she die?"

"Oh!—She died las' night."

"What was the matter with her?"

"Suh?"

"What was the matter with her?"

"Oh! I don't know, suh."

"Why didn't you send for me, or mention it before?"

"Well, you see, suh, she wuz tooken kind

o' sudden, jes las' night, an' jes went right off, so."

"They are burying her in a great hurry," said John.

"Yes, suh; looks so to me too," said Cal, sympathetically. "I specks dat ole man 'll be marryin' agin befo' de week's out. He didn' wait but two weeks las' time; I know he won't wait mo'n a week dis time." He looked the image of reprobation.

John told him he was afraid there would not be much of an attendance at the funeral, as he had heard from one of his patients that there was to be a big negro ball that night at their hall. Cal mournfully admitted that such was his fear too.

John let him go, and, taking off his coat, set to work himself.

That night a couple of John's most intimate friends dropped in just to see if he were all right, and had all his arrangements made. They found everything ready. One of them was growling about his servant having gone off to a negro ball and left his room in disorder.

"How about your wedding-suit? Is that all right? Does it fit?" they asked.

John said it was all right, and fitted perfectly. They urged him to let them see it, and finally, after much persuasion, he consented. He went to his wardrobe, and took out the box with a warm feeling about his heart, laid it tenderly on the bed, and gently opened it. It was empty.

Had his friends known the history of the suit, they would have understood his action better. For a moment John stood perfectly still, with a mystified look on his face; then he turned slowly to the wardrobe and looked through it; then he turned back to the empty box and stood over it. The next moment a string of unquotable words streamed from his lips. He wheeled suddenly, grabbed up his hat, seized a large stick from a corner and bolted out of the door.

Five minutes later a man was posted in the shadow of a tree just outside of the light of a gas lamp, a half-square from the lighted hall in which the negro ball was now going on, and close to the sidewalk along which were beginning to stream the sable attendants of the festivity. Couple after couple passed him, but the man stood in the shadow as motionless as the tree against which he was planted. A half-hour passed; the crowd was already in, and only an occasional pair came by now; still he did not budge. At last, a couple came strolling along, chatting to each other, and for the first time the shadow stirred. The voices could be heard distinctly. The man was talking.

"He couldn't git 'long at all widout me. I len's him my clo'es. I's gwine to len' him dis suit to git married in to-morrer."

The girl laughed affectedly. "Oh, shoo, Mr. Johnsing, you's jes foolin' me!"

"No, I ain't; I declare I ain't. Ef I is, I hope de debble may rise right by dat tree an'—"

He rose. The couple were right in the full glare of the lamp, Cal in a brand-new evening suit. When John stepped out, Cal could not have been more startled had his wish been literally fulfilled. He dropped the girl's arm and staggered back. Then he tried to recover himself. He stepped forward again.

"Mr. Johnny, jes le' me speak to you a minute, will you? Jes step over dis a-way a minute, won't you?"

"Take them off," said John. His voice was perfectly quiet.

"Mr. Johnny, jes—"

"Take them off," said John.

"Whar, Mr. Johnny?"

"Right where you stand," said John. He stepped a step nearer, and the light fell more fully on his face. His hickory stick was in his hand, which was squeezed tight around it till it looked knotty and white. His eyes burned like live coals. "I'll give you one minute."

"Yes, suh," said Cal, and began to hustle out of the clothes.

A dozen negroes had congregated, but neither John nor Cal took any more notice of them than if they had been in a desert.

"Now walk before me," said John. And Cal, with the clothes over his arm, walked back up the street before John as if he felt the crust of the earth breaking beneath him.

Cal came out of John's door a quarter of an hour later. John had not committed murder, but Cal knew he had had a narrow escape.

WHEN THE COLONEL WAS A DUELLIST

The question of duelling was up, and had been discussed. Most of the group were young men. Some approved the code; others were doubtful. The Colonel alone had not participated in it; he had sat through it all calmly smoking his pipe, with his head thrown back against the wall, and his eyes lazily turning from one speaker to another as the talk proceeded. Finally some one said, "Colonel, you have had a duel, of course?"

"Once." He put his pipe back into his mouth, and went on smoking again as before.

"Tell us about it," they said; for the Colonel was a man of wide experience, and of approved courage in the war. The Colonel's eyes turned up to the ceiling, and stayed so for some time, while his face took on a reminiscent expression, and when his eyes dropped again there was a look of amusement in them. He waited at least two minutes, then took his pipe out of his mouth, and emitted a cloud which would have almost concealed a mountain-top.

"Well, when I was as young and almost as big a fool as some of you are," he said, "I thought, like you, duelling was a fine thing. I had read a great deal about it, and talked more. I considered the code the proper recourse of a gentleman, and I so declared myself frequently. This did not prevent me from being disagreeable enough in other ways to get into a number of collisions, in which, as I was a strapping young fellow at the time, I was generally victorious. I was then practising law in the little county town where I started, and I deemed myself easily the greatest lawyer in the circuit, if not in the State. It was necessary to be aggressive, I thought. I had taken Lord Thurlow as my model, and I fancied myself like him. There were only two things that stood in my way: there was an older lawyer there who always treated me as if I were about three years old, and the people rather seemed to lean naturally to him. I never went into court with him that he did not make me feel like a fool. I could not pick a quarrel with him and beat him, because he was always most polite when he was most insulting, and, besides, he had only one arm, having lost the other, I had heard, in a wheat-machine. I thought he rather took advantage of it, and I used to writhe under his polished sarcasm, and lie awake at night cursing him. At last I could stand it no longer; and once, when he had gone too far for me to endure it, I consulted friends. I selected two young fellows in the village as my advisers: one, a young lawyer; the other had no profession—he was one of the best fellows in the world, but did nothing but drink whiskey. However, he was sober at that time, and as he was a great authority on the code, I felt that he would keep sober while the responsibility was upon him. I consulted them as my friends, and they advised me. The only thing as to which we differed was whether I should give my adversary an opportunity to retract. I maintained that the code required it; they disagreed with me about it. They were so indignant with him that they had taken up the notion that he was really a coward, and that I could unmask him. They seemed to me to be really blood-thirsty. I might have overcome their arguments if I had not been afraid of being thought a coward. Besides, I was rather in love with a pretty girl in the place, and I believed that a duel would make something of a hero of me, and help my cause. (If there were no women and no fools, there'd be no duels, gentlemen.)" After this parenthesis the Colonel proceeded: " Anyhow, they stood out and had their way, and a peremptory challenge was written, and intrusted to Jim Burton. It had all the vigor and venom in it that Jim and Lindman could distil. I thought it too bitter; but Lindman was a lawyer, and a challenge was a felony, anyhow. It was one of the coldest spells I ever remember; the snow was about a foot deep, and had frozen hard on top; and I well recollect how we gathered around Lindman's office fire whilst we waited for the reply to my cartel. I was afraid to go home, for we knew the row and my intention to send the challenge had got out, and the sheriff and his deputy would be after us. We barricaded the door, and pulled down the old blinds at the shutterless windows. Jim stayed so long that finally we were about to send Lindman out to look for him, when he gave the three taps agreed on at the window. He was let in, and after warming up a bit, told his story. He had had much difficulty in finding Facton—Facton was his name, I forgot to say—but had finally found him, and had presented the challenge. Facton had read it first with amusement, Jim thought; then with anger, or fear — he could not tell which. 'Fear, without doubt,' we both decided. I thought of my girl. Then he had said he would send for some one and lay the matter before him, and had told Jim he would let us hear from him in the course of a few hours.

"'Did you tell him where to send?' we asked Jim.

"'Of course,' he said. 'I told him we would sit here all night.'

"'That's right,' we agreed.

"'And he as good as kicked me out of his house, sir,' said Jim.

"'What!' We were overwhelmed at this breach of decorum, and Jim had to specify. 'Of course he did not lay his hand on me, but he rang the bell, and told that black butler of his to show me the door.' This did look like it; and Jim, who was rather talkative, declared that for a little he would call him out himself.

"'Jim, whom did he say he would send for?' we asked.

"'I did not catch the name exactly, but it sounded like "Drace"; it could not have been him, though; he's the sheriff!'

"'Drace! Are you sure it was Drace? There's only one Drace in the county, and that's the sheriff!' Jim's memory was refreshed by our repetition of the name, and he was positive it was Drace. Here was a bomb-shell. The whole plot burst on us. He was going to send for the sheriff and have us arrested, and then get the credit of being the only one out. It was diabolical. 'Why in the mischief did you tell him where we were?' we asked; which made Jim rather sulky, and he said truly that we had just praised him for doing that very thing, and said something further about our being a couple of fools. As he was necessary to us, and had done the best he could, we had to mollify him, which was not hard to do. Still, there was the question of arrest to be considered. To be the first arrested in a duel was a crying disgrace. It was decided to send Lindman out to reconnoitre. He had not been gone long when he came rushing back, and began to barricade the door faster than ever. He had run upon the sheriff himself coming out of old Facton's yard, and the sheriff had attempted to arrest him: 'But I knocked him down,' said he, triumphantly. This was a new complication. The sheriff was already the friend and creature of old Facton, who was the commonwealth's attorney, and now to have knocked him down would make him all the more bitter against us. Jim changed the current of our thoughts suddenly by saying: 'Suppose old Facton should choose shot-guns and buckshot? He's one of the best shots with a shot-gun in the world, one-armed or no one-armed.' I had not thought of this, and I was conscious of a sudden and unexplained catching of my breath which left a little taste in my mouth. Then I thought of my girl again. I asked Jim how the Colonel lost his arm. He said in the Mexican war; and I don't know why, but I was conscious again of that same sinking sensation and taste. . However, we did not have much time to consider, for just then we heard the 'cranch' of approaching footsteps through the frozen snow, and the next moment there came a thundering knock at the door, and the sheriff was demanding admittance. I was sensible of something not unlike a feeling of relief, at which I was rather ashamed, but Lindman seemed to be in a frenzy of excitement. He sprang up and seized a heavy desk. The sheriff and his posse (for there were several in the party, as we could tell from their voices), finding the door locked, dashed against it, and it creaked and cracked, and seemed about to give way, when Lindman got his desk against it and flung himself on top of it. 'Get out of the window,' he whispered; 'hurry; go to Rice's loft. I'll hold it. I'll keep the scoundrels out.' I, of course, had to appear to be trying to get away, so I began to fumble at the window, and would have found a reasonable excuse in its tight sash, if Jim had not solved the difficulty by kicking the window out, sash and all. There was nothing for me to do then but to climb out. But, Jerusalem! how cold it was! I thought the wind would split me. I was about to climb back, when Jim pushed me out. (They were the most eager seconds I ever saw.) I told them I could not go out in that wind without a hat and overcoat. They flung me a hat, and asked where my overcoat was. I was looking around with one eye for the coat and the other on the door, hoping it might give way, which it threatened to do every minute, when it did give way with a smash, and the sheriff came in head-foremost through the split. Lindman flung himself on him like a tiger, shouting to me to run — he'd hold him — and Jim gave me a shove, so there was nothing else to do, and I got out. It was as cold as Christmas, and as I ran across the lots to Rice's stable I thought the wind would cut me in two. Jim followed, and we climbed up into the loft in the hay. At first I was sensible of relief at getting out of that biting wind, but after a little I began to freeze again. I asked Jim if he thought he could get any whiskey. He said not, and began to preach on temperance in general, and especially on the necessity of sobriety in a duellist. I said, 'Jim, you talk as if you were drunk now.' He was so much offended at this that I apologized. I burrowed down into the hay, but to no purpose. Jim was better off than I, for he had an overcoat. The idea that whiskey would keep me from freezing seemed to take possession of me, and I began to think about it all the time. Presently I actually began to smell it. This rather scared me, for I thought I must be freezing to death. My feet were already numb. Jim, who had at first been very voluble, had become less and less so, and now only answered from his hole in the hay in grunts, or not at all. How long we were there I don't know, but presently I could get no answer from Jim. The idea seized me that he must be freezing to death. This, with the delusion about the smell of whiskey, aroused me, and after calling him again and again and getting no response, I crawled over to him through the dark, and put my hand on him. The first thing I struck was a whiskey-bottle. It was empty. Jim had been lying up there with that bottle until he was dead-drunk. Well, I was mad. I had a great mind to leave him there, but I was afraid he would freeze to death. My other second I knew was arrested. So there was nothing to do but to go

"'I WAS IN LINDMAN'S BED'"

in. I crawled out and took a survey. Not a light was to be seen. I was afraid to arouse any one, so I had to get Jim down out of the loft and back to Lindman's office by myself. He came down the ladder easily enough—too easily. I was afraid he had broken his neck. Did any of you ever try to carry a hundred and sixty pounds of limp humanity a quarter of a mile through a twelve-inch snow ? Well, if you have not, don't try it. Next time I'll let him freeze, if he is George Washington.

"When I got into Lindman's office the fire was out, and the door and window looked as if a cyclone had struck them. There were splinters enough, however, lying around to make a fire, and I utilized them. I soon fried Jim out enough to find he was alive ; and I never knew just how it happened, but the next thing I knew the sheriff was standing by Lindman's bed, and I was in it. He had one eye in a poultice, and his temper and nose needed one too; but, bad as they were, they were not as bad as Lindman's. Lindman had spent the night in the jail parlor, after one of the most heroical fights ever put up in the county. When he found that I had slept in his bed it capped the climax. It came near bringing on another duel, and would have done so if he could have got anybody to take his challenge that morning. As it was, we were all bound over to keep the peace, and Facton went on our bond, after making a handsome apology to me, and doing all he could to shield us from the public ridicule which threatened to overwhelm us. Lindman became his partner afterwards, and I married his daughter. That was my only duel."

The Colonel stopped, and began to reach for a match.

"What became of your old sweetheart, Colonel, for whom you fought?"

"She married a Methodist preacher, and went as a missionary to China," said the Colonel.

THE END